REA

ALLEN COUN...

P9-AGS-506

3 1833 0...

"I think I have an idea of what you need..."

Dane sincerely hoped not.

"I'll leave first," Keeley said, picking up her raincoat. "We don't want to be seen together."

"Good idea." Dane felt foolish about the cloak-and-dagger stuff, but that didn't keep him from admiring her ass as she strolled away. She paused and looked over her shoulder to catch him staring. He gave a feeble little wave and her lips curved in a small smile.

Then she pushed out the café's door and disappeared.

Dane exhaled loudly. Had Keeley tried to arouse him on purpose? If so, she'd done a good job. He did have big appetites, and not just for fine food, but for fine women.

And now he had the sneaking suspicion that he could eat a whole can of cherry filling off another woman's body and it wouldn't have the same impact on him as the earlier sight of Keeley's pink tongue licking her finger clean thanks to that cherry tartlet....

JUN 1 3 2008

Blaze™

Dear Reader,

Keeley Davis, the heroine of *Sex by the Numbers*, popped onto my computer screen as I was writing my previous book, *Bare Necessities*. One of the exotic dancers says she needs a costume receipt for her accountant, a former exotic dancer herself.

A stripper-turned-accountant intrigued me. I had no name, no physical description, only that she was a small-town girl determined to lift herself out of a difficult background. But I had just the man for her—ambitious, brawny Dane Weiss, a farm-raised, world-traveling business consultant.

Keeley is all those girls we vaguely wonder about after we leave high school—the girls of whom little is expected, except to drop out of school and work unskilled jobs. What if one of those girls surprised everyone by getting her education and a great career? A surprise to everyone except herself, because she always knew she was tough enough, smart enough and brave enough to succeed.

Here's to all the girls who make it and the people who help them!

Marie Donovan

P.S. I'm delighted to hear from my readers. Visit www.mariedonovan.com to enter fun contests and learn more about my upcoming books.

JUN 1 3 2008

SEX
BY THE
NUMBERS

Marie
Donovan

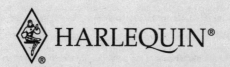

TORONTO • NEW YORK • LONDON
AMSTERDAM • PARIS • SYDNEY • HAMBURG
STOCKHOLM • ATHENS • TOKYO • MILAN • MADRID
PRAGUE • WARSAW • BUDAPEST • AUCKLAND

If you purchased this book without a cover you should be aware that this book is stolen property. It was reported as "unsold and destroyed" to the publisher, and neither the author nor the publisher has received any payment for this "stripped book."

ISBN-13: 978-0-373-79407-2
ISBN-10: 0-373-79407-X

SEX BY THE NUMBERS

Copyright © 2008 by Marie Donovan.

All rights reserved. Except for use in any review, the reproduction or utilization of this work in whole or in part in any form by any electronic, mechanical or other means, now known or hereafter invented, including xerography, photocopying and recording, or in any information storage or retrieval system, is forbidden without the written permission of the publisher, Harlequin Enterprises Limited, 225 Duncan Mill Road, Don Mills, Ontario M3B 3K9, Canada.

This is a work of fiction. Names, characters, places and incidents are either the product of the author's imagination or are used fictitiously, and any resemblance to actual persons, living or dead, business establishments, events or locales is entirely coincidental.

This edition published by arrangement with Harlequin Books S.A.

® and TM are trademarks of the publisher. Trademarks indicated with ® are registered in the United States Patent and Trademark Office, the Canadian Trade Marks Office and in other countries.

www.eHarlequin.com

Printed in U.S.A.

ABOUT THE AUTHOR

Marie Donovan, an award-winning author, is a Chicago-area native who got her fill of tragedies and unhappy endings by majoring in opera/vocal performance and Spanish literature. As an antidote to all that gloom, she read romance novels voraciously throughout college and graduate school.

Donovan has worked for a large suburban public library for the past nine years as both a cataloguer and a bilingual Spanish storytime presenter. She graduated magna cum laude with two bachelor's degrees from a Midwestern liberal arts university and speaks six languages. She enjoys reading, gardening and yoga.

Books by Marie Donovan
HARLEQUIN BLAZE
204—HER BODY OF WORK
302—HER BOOK OF PLEASURE
371—BARE NECESSITIES

Don't miss any of our special offers. Write to us at the following address for information on our newest releases.

Harlequin Reader Service
U.S.: 3010 Walden Ave., P.O. Box 1325, Buffalo, NY 14269
Canadian: P.O. Box 609, Fort Erie, Ont. L2A 5X3

To my mother, a self-made woman,
whose bravery continues to this day,
and to all the girls she's helped.

1

"ARE YOU SURE my breast implants aren't tax-deductible?" The blond bombshell sitting across from Keeley Davis tapped her acrylic nails on the rich brown maple desk. "That exotic dancer in Indiana got hers deducted and they weren't that much bigger than mine."

Keeley turned away from her laptop screen, where she was reviewing Sugar's tax return. Tax season was finally wrapping up, and none too soon for a poor, worn-out accountant. "Sorry, Sugar—it'd be a long shot. The tax court is cracking down on what they regard as frivolous deductions and I doubt we could get it past them. We can write off your costumes and the tinted latex nipple makeup, but that's about it. No personal care like tanning, manicures or hair extensions."

"And we can't appeal? I only got the implants for professional reasons, you know." Sugar pursed her pink glossy lips.

Keeley had known her friend and client too long to fall for her act. She peered over the tops of her glasses. "And you get no personal benefits from them?"

Sugar smacked her arm playfully. "Oh, all right, you naughty girl. I didn't lose any nerve sensation from the surgery and my last boyfriend and I did enjoy them."

"Thought so." Keeley pushed her glasses back up her nose to focus on the computer again. "And if we make an issue over this, the IRS might want to look in to how much of your cash tips you've been reporting as income." Keeley wasn't a novice to IRS audits, but didn't exactly enjoy them, either.

"Hmmph." Sugar backed down, like Keeley thought she would. As a certified public accountant, Keeley couldn't take part in tax evasion in the form of under-reporting garter or G-string tips, but she had a good idea that Sugar salted away her own personal cash stash, and who could blame her? Keeley would do the exact same thing in the same situation.

But Keeley was on the straight and narrow, just taking the figures Sugar gave her and plugging them into the tax program, although sometimes she raised an eyebrow at an obviously low figure. Sugar would revise it upward without blinking.

Keeley added in a couple of last-minute expenses Sugar had brought over today. Sugar, not one to sit still for any period of time, paced around the small office. Her long legs took her rapidly from one terra-cotta faux-painted wall to the other, the beige Berber carpet muffling her sneaker-clad steps. Like some dancers, Sugar had foot problems and only wore high heels onstage and on dates.

Keeley rotated her own brown-pump-clad foot under her desk. Her shoes matched her hair, her eyes, her jacket and her skirt. She was a big brown wren in comparison to her flashier blond friend, but accountants couldn't exactly sport cleavage T-shirts and midthigh denim miniskirts.

Sugar stopped to eye a pair of watercolor prints of

Florence, Italy. Keeley had never been there, but the red tile roofs matched the whole rich, Tuscan, trust-me-with-your-finances theme she wanted to emphasize. After all, accountants working in Renaissance Florence had invented double-entry bookkeeping.

Keeley printed the return and eyed it one last time before passing the pages to Sugar. "Read these over before I file electronically."

Sugar sat and speed-read through the papers. She looked as if she was skimming, but Keeley knew she was tallying every number to the penny. She finally raised her blond head and smiled. "I suppose that's as good as it gets without writing off the breast implants."

Keeley shrugged, palms upward. "If you really want me to try…"

"No, I guess not. After all, pigs get fat, but hogs get slaughtered." Sugar signed the bottom page for her own records.

"That's right." Keeley'd heard that saying more than once growing up in downstate Illinois. Not that there had been enough to even get slightly plump on. "Off it goes to Uncle Sam. Since you've made your quarterly payments, you don't owe any more than usual."

"Whoopee. I'll have to schedule myself at Frisky's a couple more nights to make up for it."

"If any of your clients work for the IRS, charge them double." And now that Keeley's highest-earning season was almost over, she'd have to save her money to make it last as long as possible until next winter.

Sugar passed the papers to Keeley. "By the way, Keel, I recommended your accounting services to an old friend of mine."

"Oh, who?" That might help tide her over while she built her client base.

Sugar grinned. "Binky Bingham."

"Boy, when you said 'old,' you weren't kidding. I thought he croaked last fall after hot-tubbing with that dancer from Chicago Gentlemen's Club." And why on earth would Binky Bingham, billionaire, need accounting services from her fledgling business?

"Alive and kicking. He's still one of her regulars, in and out of the club."

Keeley made a face. Binky fancied himself quite the ladies' man and had the money to make it so. Sugar was Binky's occasional arm candy, especially when he wanted to scare his children and grandchildren into thinking he was going to leave his money to her. He was lucky they hadn't had him declared legally incompetent and locked him up somewhere.

Sugar laughed. "Don't look at me like that. Aside from dancing for him at Frisky's, I sure never spent any time naked with him, hot tub or no."

"That's a relief." Binky Bingham was older than dirt and twice as ugly. Keeley was glad to hear Sugar hadn't slept with the old goat.

"You're telling me. Not even all of his money would be enough. For such a financial genius, he sure wasn't thinking with the right head. Viagra, a hot tub and a previous heart attack? Why didn't he just step in front of a bus? Potentially less fatal and definitely less embarrassing."

"You know Binky is incapable of embarrassment."

Sugar raised a perfectly French-manicured finger. "Personally, no. But professionally, yes. That's why

3 1833 05570 9924

your name came up." She leaned over the desk. "You absolutely cannot tell anyone what I'm going to tell you. Promise?"

Keeley narrowed her eyes. "I can't be party to anything illegal, you know that."

Her friend shook her head. "Not illegal—not so far."

"So far? Sugar, this doesn't sound good at all."

"It's about Binky's company. He thinks one of his executives is stealing money from the trust funds."

Keeley gave an astonished whistle. Bingham Brothers was the granddaddy of Chicago's financial companies, managing hundreds of millions of dollars since before the 1929 stock market crash. "It's possible, of course, but there are so many safeguards to theft. These huge companies have hundreds of people overseeing the books."

"Binky grew up with those books, and he has a gut feeling they're bad. He went into the office several times to poke around and says the atmosphere is pure poison."

"Hmmm." Keeley turned over possibilities in her mind. "Why doesn't Binky call for an audit?"

"And flush his company's reputation down the toilet? Not to mention his family's reputation. Hot-tub hijinks are one thing, but missing money is unforgivable."

Keeley nodded. A whiff of scandal and the company would bottom out. It had happened before to Chicago financial firms, usually involving bankruptcy, corporate dissolution and prison terms. "So what does Binky think I can do? I can't exactly walk in off the street and look at the books. It would take months for a whole team of auditors to examine everything."

"He has a smaller, specific group of accounts to audit

first. When I told him you'd completed a certificate in forensic accounting, his wrinkly little face just lit up. He said his representative would be in touch to get you inside for a covert audit."

"A covert audit?" Despite her misgivings, Keeley's investigative antennae perked up. She loved digging for money, ever since she was a kid checking the couch for loose change.

"So you'll do it? Binky knows absolutely everybody and can get you on the fast track if he recommends you to his friends. And you know you can bill him a bundle."

Binky would probably expect her to bill a respectable hourly consultant fee. She wouldn't gouge him, but she could legitimately bill more for doing the audit on the sly, and probably expert witness fees as well if it became a matter for the courts. Although she'd worked her way through school and had no student debt, she did have obligations. "I'll listen to what his representative says. Did he say who that is?"

"No names were mentioned, just that he was one of Binky's protégés and totally trustworthy."

Keeley snorted and Sugar giggled. Men were so naive. *Nobody* was totally trustworthy, especially when large sums of money were concerned.

"I WOULD HAVE BEEN happy to come to your office, Binky." Dane Weiss leaned over the small table to shout into his elderly friend's ear over the pulsing rock music. "Or your condo." Penthouse, rather, overlooking Lake Michigan and the rest of the city. Binky had an entire floor in Lakenheath Towers, one of Chicago's most exclusive buildings.

But Binky preferred a different kind of penthouse—the kind with naked women in it. "And miss the lunchtime show at Frisky's? At my age, I can't stay awake for the evening show." He cackled and gestured expansively to the nubile chicks cavorting above them on the runway. One flipped over and slid down a pole using just her thighs, and Dane winced. He'd never figured how they did that without friction burns, but probably some trick of the trade involving baby powder.

It wasn't as if he were a stranger to these places, having worked his way through grad school as Binky's driver/personal assistant, but he did his best to ignore the buffet of female flesh literally spread in front of him. He wasn't there for a lap dance—not that Binky would mind if he did partake.

Although the lunchtime dancers weren't quite the A-string team in their G-strings, Binky didn't care. With his overtipping, he was the life of the party. "Here, sweetheart, this is for you." He slipped a fifty into the nearest girl's garter.

Dane tried to stop him, not because Binky had to watch his pennies, but because the other girls spotted Ulysses S. Grant's bearded scowl and flocked to Binky like seagulls on a leftover sandwich. The other customers grumbled as all the entertainment clumped around the oldest and richest patron in the club.

Binky passed each of them a fifty, accepting their coos and cheek pinches. Of course the old reprobate knew them all by name.

Dane checked his watch. He'd do about anything for Binky, but sitting in a titty bar wasn't the best use of his time. Besides, Dane's fashion designer sister Bridget still occasionally made costumes for her stripper friends here and would give him hell if she caught him. Something about being a hypocrite for complaining how she had put herself through school sewing specially designed outfits for the dancers. Time to move this meeting along.

Dane raised his voice and gestured at the disgruntled mob across the runway. "Okay, girls, thanks for visiting, but we have business to discuss."

His meaning was clear. Dane figured his blond bulk helped put the point across. The dancers slinked off, Binky staring wistfully after them, his white hair mussed and cheeks marked with five different sets of lip prints.

"Dane, Dane, Dane, my boy. There is no business so urgent that one must disappoint the ladies."

Dane wanted to say that the ladies were only disappointed by not getting another fifty in their garters, but kept his comments to himself. "On the phone, you said this was urgent."

Binky sighed, his shoulders drooping. "I did invite you here for a reason—besides the entertainment. This was one of the only places I go where I am reasonably certain that none of my staff attend."

Dane nodded in agreement. Bingham Brothers was, to put it charitably, a traditional financial organization. *Hidebound* and *stuffy* were other less charitable descriptions. But despite its moldy-oldie air, it had an impeccable reputation. Binky was still the chairman of the board despite his semiretirement. "What's up, Binky?"

His friend leaned in. "I think one of my executives

is stealing from the funds entrusted to us by some of our oldest and most vulnerable clients."

That jolted Dane out of his complacency. "The trust funds?" Bingham Brothers managed money for the richest families in the nation, not just Chicago.

Binky nodded, misery apparent on his quivering lip. "It might even be Charlie."

"Charlie? Your Charlie?" Charles Andrew Bingham VI was Binky's grandson and a total prick, but Dane had never figured him for a thief. "But he's the chief financial officer. Why would Charlie steal from his own company? Doesn't he make over ten million a year?"

"It may not be the money, Dane. Charlie's always blamed me for his father's death." Binky sighed. "As if I ever had any control over Quint. Reckless, foolish boy. I thought having a son of his own would settle him, but sadly that was not to be."

Dane blew out a long breath. For Binky this wasn't only professional, it was personal. Damn. "Who else knows about this?"

"I asked a friend for advice. She's very savvy and gave me the name of a forensic accountant who can audit the accounts, if it comes to that."

"Can you trust this friend of yours not to blab?"

"Of course. Sugar Jones and I have been dear, dear friends for years." Despite his low mood, Binky managed to leer convincingly.

"Sugar Jones?" Dane fought back a groan. Sugar's mind was one giant business plan. She probably knew to the penny how much money Binky had stuffed into her garter over the years. Plus compounded interest.

"You know her?" Whoops, now Binky was getting territorial on him, like a miniature white poodle protecting a favorite squeak toy.

Dane held up his hands in a gesture of appeasement. "Purely business. She models for my sister's lingerie company."

"Lovely!" Binky beamed, his face crinkling into a map of wrinkles. Friends again. "I'll have to get her to model for me."

Dane figured modeling lingerie was more clothing than Sugar usually wore. "Binky, what do you want me to do?"

"Welcome aboard, you're my new controller-in-training."

Dane's jaw dropped. "But you already have a controller. Do you think he's involved in the missing money?"

"Glenn? No, of course not. He's wanted to retire for some time now but hasn't found a successor to his liking. Now he has."

Dane nodded. Glenn would do whatever Binky wanted. After all, Binky was still the boss.

"You're between consulting jobs, correct?"

As usual, Binky's sources were accurate. "I do have some downtime." But he planned on sleeping in for once in his life, seeing the sights of Chicago and getting laid. Not necessarily in that order.

A pretty brunette swiveled by, her legs going for miles and her long hair playing peekaboo with her firm brown nipples. She caught Dane's eye and tossed her hair back to reveal a killer pair of high, round tits.

Binky nudged him and passed him a fifty. "On me, dear boy."

Dane demurred but Binky insisted, and Dane found

himself offering the bill to the stripper, who wiggled her hips to sit on her high heels. He slipped the money into her garter, his finger skimming across her firm thigh. She ran her tongue around her lips and blew him a sultry air kiss. "Later," she mouthed and moved off when no more tips were forthcoming.

"I think she likes you!" Binky crowed.

Dane rolled his eyes. Of course she liked him, or rather liked Binky's money. He shifted uneasily on the chair and adjusted his pants. Dammit, the naked girls were finally starting to get to him.

He gave the brunette stripper's ass one last wistful gaze and turned to Binky. He owed the older man a great deal, and now was the time to pay him back. Maybe it would be a quick task to find the thief and then Dane could get to his personal business. "Okay, Binky. Tell me everything you know and how to get in touch with Sugar's friend."

Binky's shoulders slumped with relief and his brown eyes misted over. "Thank you."

Dane sighed and flipped open his BlackBerry. "You might not thank me if it turns out to be Charlie."

Binky shook his head firmly, the fun-loving roué replaced by the hard-nosed businessman. "No one steals from Bingham Brothers and gets away with it. Especially not a Bingham."

KEELEY ANSWERED her ringing phone. Good thing Sugar hadn't convinced her to play hooky after treating her to lunch at the bistro around the corner. "Hello?"

"Keeley Davis, please."

"Speaking." But just barely. The deep masculine

voice on the other end of the phone was making her speech processes a bit fuzzy.

"My name is Dane Weiss, and some mutual friends suggested we get in contact."

Ah, yes, Binky's lieutenant. Geez, he was making it sound like a blind date setup. Although if he looked as good as he sounded...back to the cloak-and-dagger stuff. "How sweet of them." She leaned heavily on the word *sweet* to see if he was quick enough to understand.

"Sweet as Sugar, if you can afford it."

She smiled at his dry tone. He'd probably met Sugar before, especially if he was a personal friend of Binky's. "And you can't afford it?"

"There are certain things a man doesn't need to pay for."

Keeley sat back in her chair and fanned her face. How true. She was about ready to give it up for this guy and she'd only been talking to him for thirty seconds. For the sake of her now-staid, CPA self, she hoped he was married, twice her age or gay. Or bald. No, bald would be fine as long as he kept talking. Well, somebody needed to keep talking. She realized their conversation had tapered off into a long, awkward pause while she'd been panting over him.

He seemed to realize the sensual bent of his words and hastened onward. "I'd like to meet with you to discuss this project. Where would be good for you?"

She could think of several places where Dane Weiss might be good for her but shoved those thoughts to the back of her mind. "You're more than welcome to come to my office."

"I'd rather we met in a social setting. This is quite sensitive material and I don't want to be seen visiting an accountant's office."

"Sure, I understand. Let's meet at the coffee shop a few blocks from my office." She gave him directions to her favorite place.

"Sounds great. How about three o'clock?"

"Today?" It was already past one.

"Definitely. I want to meet you as soon as possible."

Woof. Down, girl. "All right, three o'clock. How will I know you?" Now it really sounded like a blind date.

"I have a white shirt and red tie on today."

Yawn. So did every other businessman in the city. "What, no rose in your lapel?" Oops, her smart mouth went off again.

"No, I'll have it between my teeth." His deadpan comeback startled her into laughter. "How will I know you?"

"I have brown hair in a bun, a brown suit and glasses." Boy, that sounded boring. She frowned at her outfit. No time to go home and change. Oh, well. She was near the end of tax season and didn't have much clean laundry anyway.

"Okay, Keeley. I'll see you at three."

"See you, Dane." She hung up and drummed her nails on the desktop. No time for a manicure, either, noting her buffed natural fingertips.

Oh, well. It wasn't as if she needed stripper nails like Sugar's anyway.

2

KEELEY PUSHED through the bakery door and dangled her wet umbrella over the mat. A spring squall had broken over the city after her intriguing phone conversation and had driven rain under her umbrella, spattering her glasses and pulling damp strands of hair loose to straggle along her cheeks.

She probably looked like something the cat dragged in, but after all, accountants didn't get paid for their hairdos, just what was under it.

The teenage girl behind the counter greeted her with a slight Polish accent. Yum, she loved Eastern European bakeries. None of that low-fat, high-fiber, no-taste nonsense.

Maybe one treat. Since she was sitting at her desk more and more, she had to be careful of her carb intake. Hmm, chocolate chip cookies, donuts, sweet rolls, apple crisps and—ooh, cherry tarts. With a delicious sense of irony, she ordered the tart and a skinny latte.

She put her change in the tip jar and carried her coffee and sweet to a table on the side wall, where she could watch the door without being in its direct line of sight. A tall potted plant blocked her a bit, but she'd manage.

She placed a napkin on her lap and carefully bit into the tart, the flaky crust breaking apart on her tongue. The cherry filling was better than the usual canned pie filling, with vanilla and almond extracts mixed in. Delish. She really needed to treat herself more often. After all, a few extra minutes—or hours—on the elliptical trainer would take care of it.

Not quite three o'clock. Keeley'd have time to finish her tart and get down to business with Binky's buddy, Dane. The bell over the glass door chimed, and she peeped though the leaves like Sheena, Queen of the Jungle, sizing up her prey.

Rowrrr. A big blond guy walked in, black trench coat dripping on the floor mat. He flipped his wet hair off his forehead and wiped his eyes. Keeley couldn't exactly tell at this distance, but she guessed they were probably blue. He had the total Nordic-god, lusty-viking-raider look going on, probably several inches taller than her own five foot eleven and three quarters.

He ordered a drink and took his change with a ring-free left hand, promptly dropping the coins into the tip jar. Not a cheapskate. Then he smiled at the girl behind the counter, and dimples popped up in his cheek. She blushed and stammered, and Keeley shifted in her seat. *Come on, open that trench coat.* She wanted to see if he had a gut like other big guys often did.

As if he'd heard her mental begging, he undid his coat buttons. No way. *No way.* The trim blond hunk wearing a white shirt and red tie couldn't be Binky Bingham's right-hand man. She'd imagined some older guy in his forties or fifties who just happened to have a voice as sexy and sinful as dark chocolate.

This guy was some coffee junkie popping in for his afternoon fix.

As if he'd felt her astonished stare, he turned to meet her eyes. Keeley froze, hunter becoming the prey as he stalked toward her through the coffee shop. For a big guy, he moved easily through the maze of tables with a loose-hipped stride.

He stopped next to her table and stared at her. His eyes were blue, after all—cool blue like a spring sky. "Is this seat taken?"

As one final test, she raised an eyebrow. "I don't know. Do you have a rose?"

He grinned. "Sorry to disappoint, but it's impossible to drink coffee with a stem between my teeth."

Bingo. "Dane Weiss?" She stood and had the unusual sensation of looking well up into a man's face. A welcome change from having short guys staring into her cleavage. "Keeley Davis."

"Pleased to meet you." He set his coffee on the table and enfolded her hand in his own large one. Her fingers, almost always chilly, tingled as he warmed them. "I hope you haven't been waiting long."

Just long enough to get herself all hot and bothered. "Not at all. It was nice to get out of the office for a break. I usually push myself pretty hard."

"Me, too." He released her hand, and she missed his warmth. "Mind if I sit?"

"Be my guest." She nodded at the seat across from her. He sat on the small wooden chair, testing his size on it first before settling all the way. It looked like a child's chair under him.

"Cherry tart?"

"What do you mean?" Sugar hadn't told Binky about her, had she? She promised she wouldn't.

He gestured at her pastry. "I see you like cherry tarts."

"Oh. Yes." No reason to get defensive. "They're my favorites."

"Mine, too. I grew up on a dairy farm in Wisconsin, and we have several cherry trees in the orchard. My mom makes the best cherry jam, pies, tarts, you name it."

"I don't think I've ever had fresh cherry pie." She'd mostly grown up on snack pies her mother had brought home from the convenience store.

"You don't know what you're missing. The fruit explodes on your tongue, a bit tangy at first, but then mellowing into pure sweetness."

Keeley tried not to gape at him. My God, the man should be narrating erotica audiobooks. Cherries exploding into pure sweetness on his tongue? She really, really wanted to see that tongue in action. "You sound like you miss it. Would you like some of mine?" She pushed her plate toward him.

"Oh, no, I couldn't eat your sweets on you."

Oh, yes, he could. "Really, go ahead. It's a big tart." And so, apparently, was she. Old habits died hard.

He smiled at her the way he'd smiled at the teenage counter girl. Friendliness, but nothing more. "Just a small taste."

She didn't want friendliness. She wanted him to feel the same achy awareness that he was stirring in her. And during tax season, of all times. "Take as much as you want. Big men like you have big appetites."

He gave a quick blink at that statement, but broke off half the tart and took a bite with white teeth that had obviously received above and beyond the recommended daily allowance of dairy products. "Mmmm, not as good as Mom's, but still delicious."

"Isn't it?" She swirled her finger through the cherry filling and slowly sucked it clean. He sipped his coffee, the only hint of interest a slight flaring of his nostrils.

Good grief, the only way she could be any more obvious was if she unbuttoned her boring, off-white blouse and flashed him her rack. But she did admire self-control. Such a rare quality in a man.

DANE DRANK his coffee, hoping his rain-dampened hair would mask the fact that he'd started sweating at the sight of Keeley sucking cherry filling off her finger. "So about the project."

"Yes." She flipped open her leather-bound notepad, all business now. "Tell me what's going on."

He quietly filled her in on Binky's suspicions of his grandson and she nodded as she took notes. "I see," she began. "The subject of your investigation is the chief financial officer who has access to pretty much every account in the company, but other people obviously have access as well."

"Yeah, that's right."

"And you? Do you have access to those accounts?" She gave him a hard stare. "Any girlfriends who work there and have access to those accounts?"

He grinned. She was no fool. But if he were the thief, he would never hire a sharp cookie like her. "No, no girlfriends who work there. I've never worked there before and have had absolutely no access to any of their funds.

I will as soon as I start as acting controller, but if you take the job you'll be able to look over my shoulder and keep me on the straight and narrow."

"I was wondering how you were going to get me in. Or can you download the accounts for me to look at off-site?"

"No, you'll have to do the audit on-site. It might tip the thief off if I come on board as controller-in-training and start taking specific account information home right away."

"So I'll come in after hours and audit?"

"Not exactly." Dane took a deep breath. "Binky suggested you work at the company as my executive assistant."

She looked as if she'd swallowed a cherry pit. "You want me to be your secretary?"

"My executive assistant," he corrected, knowing semantics were futile.

"Ha. Big difference." She crumpled her napkin and tossed it on the table.

Not good. If she turned him down, he'd have to find another reputable accountant, delaying Binky's peace of mind even further. "The audit is your first priority. Believe me, I'm not going to send daily memos or write the company's annual report."

"*That* would be fun. 'Dear esteemed clients of Bingham Brothers, please disregard any minor discrepancies in your holdings. We are working diligently to discover which of our trusted executives has his or her hand in the till. Sincerely, the management.'"

He laughed. Sure, it was an awful situation, but her humor helped lighten things.

Keeley's regretful expression was obvious. "I'd

really like to help you, but I don't think it would work. I've met Charlie Bingham several times at financial networking events. I doubt he'd recognize me immediately, but he would if I spent all day in his office for several weeks."

"Damn." Dane frowned. He hadn't considered that. Leaning back in his chair to give the situation some thought, he immediately straightened when one of the legs creaked ominously. Coffeehouse chairs were either made for skinny city guys who subsisted on caffeine alone or women like the one sitting across from him.

Hmm. Under that bulky brown jacket, her tucked-in white blouse revealed a slender waist and her long skirt showed some firm calves, if not her thighs.

She cleared her throat and his gaze flew to her face. Instead of the demure blush he expected at his less-than-subtle examination, she merely looked sardonic. "Did you get a good look?"

Not hardly, but he wasn't going to say that. "Don't take this the wrong way—"

"Oh, I love it when men start a sentence with *that* disclaimer."

"Okay, okay." He backed off. "What I was going to ask, have you usually worn outfits like that when you met Charlie Bingham?"

"No, he took me to prom. Of course, he's seen my work clothes." She peered over her glasses at him as if he were an idiot, but he forged onward.

"What if you had different clothes?"

"What?"

"Not accountant clothes—younger, lighter outfits."

"More…revealing?" Her voice dipped into the husky

range. She brushed her fingers over her blouse's top button and unfastened it. She crossed her legs under the glass-topped table and hiked her skirt to her knee. She'd uncovered maybe three inches of skin in total, but Dane still found it arousing. She leaned forward, her attention totally on him. "Dane, do you want me to play dress-up for you?"

"More like a makeover," he managed to say, wondering where the sex-kitten persona had come from.

Just as quick as he wondered, she switched back to frowning CPA. "A makeover? Who do you think you are? Pygmalion? Professor Henry Higgins? The guys from *Queer Eye for the Straight Guy?*"

"Hey! I meant disguise, not makeover."

"Uh-huh."

"You know, like wearing contacts instead of glasses, maybe letting your hair down, wearing less brown…" His voice trailed off into a silent sigh. He'd handled this situation with all the finesse of the farm-fresh hayseed he used to be—or even worse, his dad's bull Caesar. "Look, I'm sorry. I understand if you don't want to take this job after this awkward beginning, but if you do want it, it's yours, disguise or no."

Her eyebrows pulled together. "You don't know me, and you're trusting me with such a big project."

"I did check you out."

"You did? And what did you find?"

"I verified your credentials, lack of criminal record, the basics."

"Ah." She nodded, relaxing the tiniest bit.

Had he missed something? His P.I. had done a routine check on her. Then he looked at her calm expression and decided to drop it. Maybe she'd gotten into trouble as a teenager, records he didn't have access to. Unless she'd done juvie time for embezzlement, he didn't really care. "And Sugar's recommendation carries a lot of weight. That woman is a walking financial calculator."

Instead of reassuring her, she frowned again. "How do you know Sugar?"

Ah, she was probably wondering if he was one of Sugar's lap-dance clients. "Not from her work, at least not directly. She models for my sister Bridget's lingerie line."

She grinned. "Oh, yes. 'Bras by Brigitte.'"

"Yeah. That's it." Silly fake-French marketing ploy, but sales were taking off.

"I'll have to look for some of her designs when I'm shopping. For my makeover."

It took him a second. "You mean you'll do it? That's great!"

She raised a slim hand. "Don't get all excited yet. Binky Bingham is going to pay me big-time."

"Hey, he wouldn't expect anything less." Binky was used to paying women lots of money.

Her next words proved she knew Binky's habits as well. "I don't accept cash, especially tightly rolled fifties. He can write me checks at the beginning, middle and end of the audit, with additional billing if I get involved in legal proceedings."

"And he'll pay for any clothing you may need to do the job."

She raised an eyebrow. "A clothing allowance? Maybe I *will* get one of your sister's pricey bras. Sugar says they're so comfortable, you practically feel naked."

A naked Keeley? Images of Keeley undressed like

the brunette stripper from Frisky's tumbled around his head. He never mixed business with pleasure, and Binky's business was important. Dane didn't need to ask himself what was wrong—he already knew.

"Dane?" Her questioning voice broke into his confusion. "Here, take a napkin before your pants get stained."

"What?" He looked in horror at the paper napkin she offered him. Sure, she was turning him on, but he wasn't even close to staining anything.

With an exasperated sigh, she dropped the napkin on the table in front of him and soaked up a puddle of coffee. "Your cup is leaking."

"Oh." He didn't realize he'd crumpled his paper cup while imagining her naked. He grabbed more napkins and mopped the mess. Lucky he'd almost finished his coffee. "So, Keeley. Tax season is almost over. When can you start working at Bingham Brothers?"

"April fifteen is next Wednesday. After that, I need a couple days off to shop and catch up on my sleep. I've been getting by on four or five hours a night, and I want to spend all day in bed if I feel like it."

Boy, did he feel like spending all day in bed with her. He nodded brusquely. "Will the following Monday work for you?"

"Monday, it is."

"Good. I'll courier over a check for your advance and clothing allowance, and I'll expect you at 8:00 a.m. sharp at Bingham Brothers. Wear your new clothes."

She raised an eyebrow. "Yes, sir, Mr. Weiss. I'll practice my shorthand over the weekend in case you want to give me your dictation."

Man, did she have to use that word? "Not necessary." He passed her his business card. "My cell number's on the front. Call me with any questions."

"I think I have an idea of what you need."

He sincerely hoped not.

She stood, shimmied her skirt to midcalf and picked up her raincoat. He rose and they shook hands again. "I'll leave first. We don't want to be seen together."

"Good idea." He felt foolish about the cloak-and-dagger stuff but that didn't keep him from admiring her ass as she strolled away. Her plain brown pumps had enough of a heel to add just the right amount of wiggle, and the watery sunlight lit the strands of caramel-colored hair that escaped from her bun. She paused before opening the door and looked over her shoulder to catch him staring. He gave a feeble little wave and her lips curved in a small smile.

Then she pushed out the door and disappeared among the busy pedestrian traffic.

Dane exhaled loudly. Had Keeley been trying to arouse him on purpose? If so, she'd done a good job. Talking about his big appetites hadn't helped any, either. He did have big appetites, and not just for fine food, but for fine women.

But now he had the sneaking suspicion that he could eat a whole can of cherry filling off another woman's naked body, and that wouldn't have the same impact on him as the sight of Keeley's pink tongue licking her finger clean. Dammit, dammit, dammit.

3

"CONTROLLER-IN-TRAINING for Bingham Brothers?" Dane's best friend and future brother-in-law Adam Hale drank his dark Guinness beer and raised a black eyebrow.

"Yep. Binky Bingham offered me the job a few days ago and I accepted. I moved my stuff into one of their corporate apartments until I find a permanent place." Or until the audit was finished and Dane could move on. He gestured to the bartender to bring him another bottle of Wölfbräu, a Wisconsin beer brewed not too far from his parents' farm. He was drinking the original brew because that was what the bar carried, but his favorite variety was Wolfie's Honey Weiss, a honey-flavored pale ale.

Adam shook his head. "I have to admit, I can't see you working permanently for any company, much less them. I thought Charlie Bingham tried to punch you once." Adam was a financial analyst for another big Chicago company and knew the local heavy hitters.

"Yeah, the keyword is *tried*." Dane drank some beer and they both laughed. Charlie Bingham was a health club monkey, good for swinging off the bars but not much else. "I was attending the same charity function as his grandfather and Charlie made a drunken crack about Binky's date."

"Probably younger than Charlie," Adam commented. "Still, not the thing to do to your family, especially in public."

"He was upsetting Binky, so I said something to him and he took a swing at my jaw. He missed by a mile, so I pinned his arm behind his back and poured him into his limo to go sleep it off."

"Gee, Dane, I can see why you'd jump at the chance to work there. Sixty-hour weeks in some bland office, fossilized business practices and a chief financial officer who'll stab you in the back with his secretary's letter opener if you drop your guard. A real dream job compared to your last few months freelancing for that up-and-coming Asian firm." Adam rolled his eyes. "Come on, what's up?"

Dane munched on some peanuts and considered what to say to Adam, who was part of the same industry and not uninterested in such an eminent company. Family or no, Binky's confidentiality came first. "Binky asked me to come aboard. He's not getting any younger, you know."

"He's not, but his dates are!" Adam caught Dane's warning glance and grinned. "Okay, okay. I know Binky took you under his wing when you were a broke MBA student."

"I owe him a lot, and now it's time to pay him back." His tone indicated it was a closed subject.

"Okay, Dane." Adam reached for some pretzels and gazed at the baseball game on the TV. They were in a bar where the guys from the neighborhood stopped for a few brews before heading home. Despite Adam's polished city-boy appearance, he came from a similar blue-collar background. "Geez, would you look at that?

The Brewers are losing to the Cubs again. Pathetic." He turned to Dane. "Well, Binky's lucky to have someone like you at his side. Men in his position often don't have any allies without their own agendas. You're a loyal man."

Loyal? Dane supposed he was, although he'd never thought of it that way. Loyal, dependable Dane. Not the most exciting description, but it beat being a rude jerk like Charlie.

What kind of man did Keeley like? Over the past several days since their coffee meeting, he'd caught himself looking forward to seeing her tomorrow morning. He hoped she'd bought some outfits that showed off her body a bit more. If Charlie thought she was only working there because Dane was interested in her, Charlie would have even more reason to drop his guard.

As long as Dane didn't drop his. Problem was, he could instantly imagine Keeley taking his "dictation" naked and flat on her back on the conference table. Or maybe in the copier room against some paper cartons. Or sitting in a big leather office chair, her ankles draped over the arms.

He didn't know why he was so attracted to her, considering he usually went for women who were obviously sexy and not afraid to show it. Maybe it was those flashes of sex-kittenhood popping out from her buttoned-up accountant persona. And the way she swung her ass from side to side when she absolutely *had* to know he was watching her. He rubbed his hand across his face.

"You okay?" Adam nudged his elbow. "You're all red."

"Am I?" He knew he was, judging from the heat in his cheeks. "Kind of warm in here."

"If you say so." The bar's air-conditioning was turned to frigid temperatures thanks to a mid-April heat wave. Fortunately, his friend let it drop. "Bridget will be glad you're going to stay in Chicago for a while. You can help us plan the wedding."

"Oh, goody, can I?" Dane gave him a sidelong glance. It had taken some getting used to that his baby sister was living with and would be marrying Adam, Dane's former bar buddy and champion chick-scoring wingman.

Adam cleared his throat. "After all, we want you to be my best man. You and your brother, that is."

"Colin and me? Are you sure you want me? After all, I did try to strangle you when I learned you were dating Bridget." More than just dating actually, but those events were better left unmentioned.

"Hey, what's a little strangulation between brothers?" Adam joked, but his dark eyes were serious.

"Adam, ever since you and Colin were roommates at college, I've always thought of you as a brother. Marrying Bridget just makes it official."

Adam swallowed hard and clapped him on the shoulder. "Thanks, buddy."

"No problem." Dane nodded and slapped him on the back in return. Okay, big emotional moment over. Maybe they could catch the end of the ball game.

"You know, this engagement and marriage thing is pretty cool."

Dane gave a quiet sigh. Back to the emotional stuff. "Yep."

"I mean, after all these years of knowing you guys and knowing your sister and having it all come together so we're all together—it's pretty cool." Adam grinned like a goofball.

"Cool," he agreed. Cool, if incoherent. What inning was the ball game in, anyway?

"Now that you're staying put for more than one week, maybe you can meet someone, too."

That got his attention. "Geez, Adam. Don't go all squirrelly on me. I'm glad for you two, but now is not the right time in my life to go looking for anyone." Adam would soon know that Dane's time in Chicago would only be long enough to finish his investigation and move on. Dane already had some feelers out for his next consulting job.

"Love comes when you least expect it," Adam intoned, the beige Guinness foam on his upper lip ruining the sentiment.

"What are you, a greeting card poet?" Dane shook his head. Adam had to be drunk to spout such sappy crap.

His friend smirked. "Laugh if you want, but you know the old saying—the bigger they are, the harder they fall. And you are one big guy."

"That refers to being punched in the jaw, not falling in love."

Adam grinned and socked him in the shoulder. "Take it from me. You won't be able to tell the difference."

"WHAT SHOULD WE DRINK TO?" Sugar hoisted her butterscotch-vanilla martini high in anticipation.

Keeley lifted her *limoncello* cocktail in response. "To the end of tax season!"

"To the start of a new tax year with lots more money!" Sugar slugged back her drink and Keeley followed suit, the tart liquor puckering her lips. Yum.

The trendy bar they were drinking in made the coolest cocktails. Since it was Sunday night, the crowd was a bit lighter, but more casual than Friday or Saturday night. The weekend was basically over, so people were more relaxed and not trying so hard to hook up with each other.

"Thanks for treating me to dinner and drinks, Keeley. It's fun to get dressed for a girls' night out. I got stuck working Friday night and last night, so I could use a break before my Monday morning class."

"Thanks for suggesting we come here, and you're welcome. It's the least I could do after you treated me to lunch last week." After getting Binky's first check, she had a bit of breathing room.

"But that was lunch, not dinner and drinks. You must have had a great tax season. Or maybe Binky's gig panned out and you're doing his audit?" Sugar swiped some butterscotch sauce off the rim of her martini glass and licked her finger.

Keeley hesitated, client confidentiality keeping her from spilling her guts.

"Oh, come on, Keel. You know Binky tells me everything." She dug in her purse and held up her cell phone. "I can call him to give you permission if that would make you feel better."

"If you want to know that badly, go ahead."

Sugar pressed a couple buttons, and Binky's name popped up on her phone screen.

"He's on your speed dial?" Keeley whispered.

"Anyone with eight or nine zeroes in his bank account is on my speed dial," Sugar whispered. "Hello, Binks, sweetie, how are you?"

Binky was apparently fine and wanted to tell Sugar all about it. Keeley slugged back the rest of her *limoncello* while Sugar made appropriate cooing noises. That was the trouble with dancers seeing customers outside of the club. They got way too involved with each other's personal lives, and things could get messy. On the other hand, Binky's fraternization with strippers had landed Keeley a job with him, so who was she to complain?

"Binky, I'm here with my good friend Keeley, but she's superprofessional and won't tell me a *thing* about your situation until you give her the green light." She listened and handed the phone to Keeley. "He wants to talk to you."

"Hello?"

"Binky Bingham, here. Please feel free to take Sugar into your confidence, my dear. She has one of the best business brains I've run in to. In fact, on that unfortunate day when she steps down from her entertaining career, I've told her she can have carte blanche of positions at Bingham Brothers."

"Thank you, Mr. Bingham. I take my clients' confidentiality very seriously—"

"Of course you do. Could you ask Sugar when she's next scheduled to perform at Frisky's?"

Keeley rolled her eyes but did as he asked.

"Wednesday. I'll be looking for you, Binky!" she called into the phone.

"Excellent. Goodbye, and good luck, Kelly." Binky hung up.

Close enough, as long as his check cleared.

"So who is Binky's mysterious protégé?" Sugar leaned closer over her glass.

"You know him—Dane Weiss. I start working with him at Bingham Brothers tomorrow."

"My, oh, my, Bridget's brother!" Sugar whistled. "And how is the very virile viking these days?"

Keeley wondered if Sugar had ever been close to Dane's "virility." "You know him well, then?"

"I've met him a few times at Bridget's functions, but never outside that." She giggled and wiggled her perfectly groomed eyebrows. "Don't worry, sweetie. He's not a regular of mine. In fact, he thinks I'm a bad influence on his sweet little sis. She came to Chicago fresh from the family farm and fell in to designing stripper outfits for rent money. Of course, that's how she got her big break, but that's neither here nor there to him. He disapproves of the whole business."

"Dane doesn't like strippers and he's a friend of Binky's?" Keeley asked skeptically. "Binky does enough business at Frisky's to list their address on his tax return."

"Yeah, considering how much money he spends there, Tony the manager would offer Binky a lap dance himself to keep him happy."

Keeley shuddered at the idea of short, fat Tony gyrating above Binky in his shiny gray suit and open-neck black shirt, his gold chains glittering. "I need another drink to get that picture out of my mind."

Sugar hailed the waiter, who practically vaulted over three tables to get to her. He took their reorder and galloped back with their drinks.

Keeley took a sip of her *limoncello* cocktail. She loved the fresh lemon liqueur, a grown-up version of the *el cheapo* powdered lemonade she and her sister drank on hot summer days when they were kids. Lacey used to set up elaborate lemonade stands for the neighborhood kids while Keeley kept a protective eye on her. At least the lemonade stand had never been robbed, unlike the convenience store where their mom worked.

Dane Weiss had grown up on a dairy farm. She bet he never had to worry if his dad was going to come home from the barn or if a cow would pull a pistol on him.

"That was a pretty heavy sigh, Keel." Sugar, an expert at reading people's moods, eyed her over her martini rim. "Don't worry about this gig with Dane. He's a real straight shooter."

Keeley shook her head. "If he's such a straight shooter, I don't know how this will all turn out." She leaned over the table. "I'm going in undercover as his secretary."

"Undercover or under the covers with Dane?" Sugar whooped.

"Ha, ha." Although she had definitely considered the second possibility. Dane was so big, so strong and handsome… She drank most of her *limoncello* to try to cool off.

"If you don't want him, I'll give him another try. Maybe he likes blondes."

"Hands off, honey," Keeley snapped without thinking.

Sugar giggled. "Well, well. I haven't heard that tone of voice from you in a long time."

"Just slipped out," she mumbled. And she couldn't even blame the cocktails, since it was only her second.

"Keeley, darling, please put yourself first for once. Ever since we've known each other, you've been all work and no play. Helping your sister, putting yourself through school and finally taking that dreadful CPA exam—how many hours was it?"

"Fifteen long, torturous hours sitting in front of a computer terminal."

"Ugh." Sugar shuddered. "And I thought my MBA classes were bad. So when was the last time you got any?"

"Any what? Sleep?" Sugar was right. She had been going nonstop for months.

"You know *what.*"

"Oh, *that. That's* been kind of low on my priority list lately."

"Well, rewrite your priority list with *that* at the top. You could do worse than Dane Weiss to have some fun with. He's single, handsome and really strong from that clean, dairy-farm upbringing. He's built like a bull."

"And probably hung like one, too," Keeley answered without thinking. She'd seen a bit of a wiggle under his zipper during her double entendres at the bakery.

"There you go!" Sugar patted her hand. "Thank goodness, a sign of life after all."

"I don't know, Sugar. I'll be working with him for several weeks and it could be awkward bringing sex into the equation."

"Nonsense. It'll add to the spice. Fear of discovery is a major turn-on for men. You know that."

Keeley did know that. Could she put herself first for once? And would Dane even be receptive to her? "I don't know. Maybe he won't be interested in me. Maybe I've lost my touch."

"Puh-leeze! Once you've got it, you never lose it. Ditch those boring brown dust rags you call clothes and lighten up. Just because you're an accountant doesn't mean you have to dress like a manila file folder."

"That's what Dane said. In fact, Binky's paying me a clothing allowance to disguise myself so Charlie won't recognize me from previous networking events."

"Clothing allowance?" Sugar straightened. "How much?"

"A bundle. But I haven't had time to spend it since I got stuck filing a bunch of tax extensions this weekend. I do have enough old outfits to get me through a few days at Bingham Brothers."

"Your old outfits?" Sugar raised her eyebrow.

"I still fit in them, you know." Geez, it wasn't as if she'd porked up.

"Not exactly office wear."

"I know that. Nobody will suspect the newest bimbo secretary of auditing the accounts, and besides, Dane told me to wear more revealing clothing." He had no idea what he was in for tomorrow.

"Dane's the boss. I know you'll knock his socks off."

Keeley drained her glass. "Maybe I'll knock his pants off instead."

KEELEY UNLOCKED the door to her second-floor walk-up apartment and hung her waist-length brown leather jacket on a hook in the narrow foyer. She walked into the small kitchen with its metal 1950s cabinets and tossed her keys on the gold-speckled Formica counter.

Her vintage 1905 greystone was one of the few buildings left untouched by the renovation bug sweeping through the Ukrainian Village neighborhood. Her landlady lived downstairs and had successfully resisted her sons' attempts to move her into an assisted living home and sell out to a rehabber. Of course, once everything was overdeveloped, Ukrainian Village would lose the qualities that made it a fun place to live—reasonable rents, decent parking and a laid-back, yet hip atmosphere.

Keeley grabbed a bottle of water from the fridge and headed into the bedroom to decide what on earth to wear on her first day as an undercover bimbo.

She opened the tiny closet and reached past the white-and-cream high-neck blouses, brown, black and gray suits, and the sensible neutral pumps and subdued silk scarves, to the clothes she never wore anymore, but hadn't been able to let go of.

She pulled out skintight sleeveless tops in fuchsia, red and lime-green, skirts so short they were illegal in certain jurisdictions and the literal kicker, four-inch high stilettos and platform heels in black, white and clear plastic Lucite.

If bimbos ever got together and wrote a dress code, she could comply perfectly. She stripped off her khaki pants and cream-colored blouse and exchanged them for a low-cut white top, black miniskirt and black open-toed heels with rhinestone ankle straps.

She took a few experimental steps across her bedroom, her old sashay falling into place. The heels were higher than she was used to, but the rhinestones still sparkled nicely, if not as much as they had under the stage lights.

She stopped in front of the mirror. Something was out of place. The clothes were okay, her bod still fairly decent, but it was the hair. Too brunette.

She reached up to the top shelf—easy to do in her

platforms—and picked a round white box. Blowing the dust off, she set it on her bed and studied her emphatic hot-pink printing on the top. *Property of Cherry Tarte!!!* She shook her head at the juvenile writing. At least she hadn't drawn hearts to dot the exclamation points.

She removed the lid and lifted out her absolutely favorite red-haired wig, its luxuriant waves cascading over her hands. Brenda Starr-red. Rita Hayworth-red. Ann-Margret-red. And of course, stripper-red.

Pulling the wig on, she tucked her hair under it and stared at her reflection. "Hello again, Cherry," she said to herself. "Bet you thought you'd never come out of retirement."

For it had been the infamous Cherry Tarte, Keeley's alter ego, who had paid for her accounting degree by baring it all for the boys at the Love Shack. It was ironic, to say the least, that she'd use Cherry's persona for what could be the biggest accounting job of her career.

And it was all thanks to Dane Weiss and his need for a bimbo forensic accountant. She couldn't wait to see his face when his new executive assistant started work tomorrow morning all tarted up. Or rather, "Cherry-Tarted."

4

RUNNING LATE WAS not the way Dane wanted to start his pseudocareer at Bingham Brothers, but he'd stayed awake late going over the background materials from Binky. Probably a whole lotta nothing, but he always needed to know about the major players before he walked into a new place.

Dane paid the cabbie in front of the LaSalle Street skyscraper that housed Bingham Brothers and punched the elevator button to take him to the offices on the upper floors.

It was a long elevator ride, and he yawned, partly to pop his ears and partly because he needed to. Even after he went to bed, he'd dreamed of the brunette stripper from Frisky's. Not particularly unusual for a guy who'd been celibate for a few months, but the part that had really woken him up sweating and hard was when she turned to face him. It had been Keeley Davis looking at him with a sexy, come-hither look.

And he was the guy who had asked her to dress sexier for the office? Granted, it was to fool Charlie Bingham, but Dane was the one who would be working with her fifty or sixty hours a week.

The elevator doors opened and he stepped into the

cool gray lobby of Bingham Brothers and approached the middle-aged receptionist with her apricot helmet of hair. No teenage, nail-filing receptionists for them. This lady had probably been the company's telephone operator since the age of plug-in switchboards.

"May I help you, sir?"

Dane introduced himself and quickly found himself in possession of a photo ID badge and directions to his new office. She showed him how to swipe himself in through the security system and, presumably, the time clock as well.

He thanked her and passed into the offices, threading through several columns of cubicles and pushing through the door marked with his name. He stopped in surprise.

A mob of guys stood around the desk where, he surmised, Keeley sat. Judging by the way their backs were to him, he guessed they weren't waiting to greet him with a rounding chorus of "For He's a Jolly Good Fellow." Unless she was running the office betting pool, Dane would gamble that they were all chatting her up.

"Good morning." His loud tone cut through the noise. The men jumped away guiltily, parting like the Red Sea to reveal a redhead. And what a redhead she was…her long, glorious waves falling over her shoulders and her breasts, brushing the edges of some Grand Canyon-deep cleavage flashing from a tight, white blouse.

Where was Keeley?

"Good morning, Mr. Weiss," the redhead purred.

Oh, dear God, it *was* Keeley. She'd made her hazel eyes look wider and greener, her coy brushing of eyelashes dark on her cheek. She even had a little Cindy

Crawford mole near the corner of her mouth. Real or drawn on, he didn't care. It was a point on a map, leading the way to her full, red lips.

She smiled at the men flanking her. "Sorry, boys, playtime's over. Looks like the boss is here."

Her husky tones rolled over the male crowd, pulling them further into her spell. He had to clear his throat and glare pointedly at the outer door. They straggled out, some giving him nasty looks, some gazing longingly at her. He was sure to be one popular guy at Bingham Brothers.

He grabbed Keeley's elbow and steered her into his inner office. Holy cow, where was the rest of her skirt? She had to have at least twelve inches of visible thigh. Her black micro-micro mini barely covered her ass when she was standing. If he started at her knee and stroked upward on those firm, toned thighs, he could slip his hand under that skirt with room to spare.

"Good morning, Mr. Weiss. I'm your new assistant, Cherry," she singsonged. "How do you take your coffee?"

Ice-cold and down his pants, that's how. "What the hell is this getup?"

"Exactly what you asked for—younger and lighter. Nonaccountant clothes."

He sat on the edge of his desk, flabbergasted. Yeah, he'd asked for it, all right. But what had he gotten? "You're so far from accountancy, you're not even the same species. Where on earth did you get that outfit?"

"A little something I had in the back of my closet."

"Yeah, right. Where'd you go shopping, the stripper store?"

"You mean the store where your sister gets her design ideas?" Her tone was syrupy sweet.

He rubbed his jaw. She had him there. "Okay. But attracting attention wasn't what I had in mind." He lowered his voice and leaned over to her. "How are you supposed to conduct a covert audit when nobody can take his eyes off you?"

"That's the plan." She gave him a sly smile. "It's like a magician's sleight of hand. You distract the audience with flashy stuff on top while the serious business goes on below."

"Flashy stuff on top?" His gaze was drawn to the low-cut vee of her blouse. Her cleavage had some kind of gold glitter lotion highlighting the full curves of her breasts. The lotion was perfumed, too, as he greedily inhaled her warm, sexy scent.

The base of her throat moved as she swallowed hard. "Dane?" She snapped her fingers in front of his line of sight and pointed to her face. "Up here."

He grudgingly looked up and eased away from her. "Sorry about that. Your plan worked too well on me."

"Yeah, well, you're a man, aren't you?"

Her deprecating tone rubbed him raw. "Some men, like me, for example, can think of other things besides 'flashy stuff on top.'" He could, couldn't he?

"Funny, Sugar didn't mention you were gay. Not that there's anything wrong with that." She gave him a sympathetic look.

He was speechless for several seconds. Gay? She thought he might be gay? Then he saw the corners of her full red lips pull into a tiny smirk. Ah, playing games with him. Well, he could play, too. "No, I'm not gay. I just go for a different type of woman. No offense to you, of course."

"None taken." Her smirk disappeared as quickly as her clothing in his imagination. "So what type do you go for?" she asked.

"Um…" He couldn't very well tell her the truth, which was that he liked tall, leggy brunettes. And tall, leggy redheads. "Petite blondes." That would get her good. According to his sister, tall brunettes always hated short blondes, especially when short blondes took all the tall guys. And he was tall.

She curled her lip delicately. "And you don't get a crick in your neck bending over those petite blondes?"

He shrugged. "Not everything is done standing. But anyway, time to get to work, *Cherry*. See if you can't find a pad of paper so we can make some notes."

Keeley didn't quite stomp off to her desk, but her gait was definitely stiff. He eased into his chair so she couldn't see how her tight ass in the tiny skirt was making him stiff, too.

"PETITE BLONDES, my ass." Keeley yanked open her desk drawer and found a yellow legal pad. *Not everything is done standing.* That big ox would squash one like a blond bug. She hoped he stayed awake long enough after sex to let the girl roll clear. She bet Dane liked being on top. Bossy guys often did, until they were shown the advantages of being on bottom.

Her nipples tightened under her thin white top and her black thong was becoming suspiciously moist. Hmm. Maybe thinking about how Dane liked to have sex wasn't the best way to spend her first morning at the office.

And he was waiting for her. She grabbed a felt-tip pen so as not to leave indentations in the paper below.

The old trick of rubbing pencil over the pressed-in marks still worked, and she didn't trust anyone here.

She closed the drawer, but before she could return to the office, trouble arrived in a two-thousand-dollar suit.

"And you are?" Charlie Bingham raised a black brow.

Good morning to you, too, creep. "I am Cherry…" Shoot, she'd forgotten to think of a last name for her alias. She'd never needed one before. "Cherry Smith."

"Cherry? How…interesting." His tone implied that Cherry was the goofiest name ever. As if he hadn't lost his virginity to some snooty broad named Buffy, Muffy or Trixie. "And you actually work *here?* At Bingham Brothers?"

"Yes, indeed. I'm the executive assistant to the new controller-in-training."

"Dane Weiss." He said that with the same lip curl as someone would say "dog doo."

Dane moved next to her, his presence an instant comfort. How long had it been since anyone had backed her up? "Good morning, Charlie. I see you've met my executive assistant, Cherry."

Binky's grandson gave her an insolent once-over. Rude little shit. She took a great deal of pleasure in looking down at him from her towering Lucite high heels.

"Why am I not surprised, Weiss? Trust you to find the flashiest assistant possible." He laid on the word *assistant* with a snotty tone.

Keeley fought the urge to roll her eyes since she'd heard it all before, and from nastier specimens than him, but what was interesting was Dane's reaction. A flush roiled up his neck and onto his face, the tips of his ears reddening. Was he embarrassed?

Then she saw his clenching fists. Nope, angry. Really angry.

"This young lady is my executive assistant. You may call her Miss, uh…"

"Smith," Keeley supplied.

"Or better yet, don't call her anything at all. If you have something to say, you tell me, instead of bothering her with your bad attitude, Charlie."

Keeley's eyes widened so fast her fake eyelashes popped loose at the edges. Dane was defending flashy, trashy Cherry. How sweet.

"Don't call me Charlie!" The dark-haired man was turning a matching shade of red. "My name is Charles Andrew Bingham the Sixth, and you call me Mr. Bingham, dammit!"

"Mr. Bingham is your grandfather, Charles Andrew the Sixth. Maybe I'll call you Chuck."

Keeley smothered a grin at the outraged expression on Charlie's face. Chuck was even worse than Charlie.

"I'm on to you, Weiss," he said, hissing Dane's last name. "You think you can waltz in here and con my senile coot of a grandfather, but you can't fool me. You're up to something, and I'll keep my eyes on you until I find out exactly what." He shot his fancy French cuffs and strode out of the office.

Keeley laughed. "Way to fly under the radar, Dane. I thought for a second the two of you were going to have a real honest pissing contest here in the office."

Dane spun back to her, the blood sinking from his face and returning it to his normal color. "We've had words before."

"No!" She pressed her hand to her bosom in mock surprise. "And here I thought you had a special gift for making friends and influencing people. Or didn't they teach you that in business school?"

He motioned her into his office and closed the door. "Chuckles was rude to his grandpa and his grandpa's lady friend. I gave him a brushup on the rules of etiquette."

Probably Binky's date was Sugar or one of her friends. "Good grief. How many stitches did he need?"

"None."

"X-rays?"

"None."

"Clean pairs of underwear once he got home?"

Dane burst out laughing. "None. Really, he took a poke at me and I shoved him into a limo."

"Too bad. I'm sure he must have deserved a butt-kicking at various points in his life."

"Sorry." He extended his palms upward. "He's still Binky's grandson."

"And our only suspect at this point," she murmured.

"Yep." Dane quirked a corner of his mouth. Yikes, the man's dimples were lethal.

She brandished her felt-tip pen. "Despite your reservations, my disguise worked. There's no way Charlie's going to think I'm anyone but some bimbo secretary you're boffing."

"True. You're no bimbo secretary."

Keeley waited for him to respond to the part about boffing, but he just gave her a slow, lazy smile. "Let's get to work, shall we? We'll leave the boffing discussion for another time."

"DANE WEISS'S office, may I help you?" Keeley stuck out her tongue at the sultry female voice on the other end requesting a lunch meeting with Dane. It was yet one more female upper-management type panting after him. Over the past week, Dane had enough lunch invitations to eat seven times a day.

"I'm sorry, Mr. Weiss is tied up with meetings the rest of the week." She had no idea whether or not he was, but there was no way he was going for three-hour lunches while she was stuck in the office.

She and Dane had been in Bingham Brothers orientation for several days with no access at all to the accounts. If she had to sit through another PowerPoint presentation on company culture, she'd throw one of her lethal shoes straight through the projection screen.

When she hadn't been pinching herself to keep awake, she'd surfed the company's intranet to familiarize herself with the antiquated accounting systems, policies and procedures.

"Who was that?" Dane leaned against the doorjamb, his arms crossed over his chest. Today he had on a navy-blue shirt that really brought out his eyes.

She hadn't bothered to note the woman's name and had forgotten it as soon as the receiver clicked. "She'll call back if it's important."

He laughed. "Suzanne in accounting and Barbara in human resources each told me they wanted to have a lunch meeting with me when my schedule cleared. I didn't know my schedule was that full."

"That's why *I'm* here, Mr. Weiss, so you don't need to worry your important self about your schedule." She threw back her shoulders in her low-cut black blouse and shook her fake red mane.

He closed the outer office door. "Some people might think you're trying to keep me all for yourself."

Was she? Despite her big talk to Sugar, Keeley'd had reservations about getting involved sexually with Dane Weiss while she was working for him. Maybe her disobedient subconscious was butting in again. "And some people, like me, want to get started with *other* important projects. Some people are tired of getting air-conditioning drafts blown up their office-inappropriate clothing."

He shook his head and smiled. "I hope your clothing allowance is enough to hold you over."

"Like I told you, I got these from the back of my closet."

"Right, right." He winked, obviously not believing her. "Well, if you need more shopping money, let me know."

"I'm good, thanks." She probably had another six or eight outfits she hadn't worn yet. "Hope you like lime-green and fuchsia."

"Together?" He looked confused.

"Hardly. I'm dressing a bit flashy, not like a circus clown."

"The sacrifices we make for our careers. And here's another one. Now that Glenn, the current controller, feels I'm up to speed, I've been cleared to have account access. We're going to have some late evenings this week, starting tonight."

Working late with Dane? A little shiver ran through her. "Here at the office?"

"Yep. We need to start with your bean-counting magic."

"What if I have a hot date tonight?" She didn't, but wanted to keep him on his toes.

"I wouldn't be surprised, considering the way you look." He leaned down. "I knew you'd be a distraction the second I saw you sitting behind this desk."

"You did?" Whose breathy voice was that? Okay, now her subconscious had knocked her conscious unconscious and locked it in the supply closet.

"Every morning, I have to chase at least three or four guys out of here. You're never going to be able to get anything done during regular hours."

So she didn't distract him? She wasn't so sure about that. "I guess I'll have to cancel my date. Disappointing, but I'll survive."

"I'll make it up to you." He passed her chair on his way to his desk.

She couldn't help sneaking an eye-level glance at his ass, the cheeks flexing under his thin Italian charcoal wool trousers. "How?"

He stopped, giving her a good view of his zipper. Oh, for X-ray vision. "Order in whatever you'd like and I'll have the same."

"You're on. I'll have it delivered at six."

"Good. We'll work in the corner conference room." He continued into his office and was quickly engrossed in the contents of his laptop screen.

Keeley turned back to her own computer and noted the time at the little clock in the corner. Not even lunchtime yet. Suddenly, six o'clock seemed a long way off. She snuck a glance at Dane, his blond brows drawing together as he focused on whatever he was looking at.

She only wished he'd paid that much attention to her. Oh, he'd been friendly and polite to her the past week they'd been working together. Considering her over-the-top, not-much-on-top clothing, she'd half expected him to be part of the parade of drooling numbskulls traipsing through her office on the stupidest of pretexts. Did Cherry have a stapler to borrow? Did Cherry have any pink sticky notes? Did Cherry need a can of pop from the break room?

Cherry didn't need a thing. It was Keeley who needed a ton of things. She needed to get started on her audit, needed the money from Binky to help pay Lacey's dorm bill for next fall, and needed to get a life somewhere along the way.

Thinking, she bounced her pencil eraser on the desk. Despite the fact that she'd regularly pranced around in front of strange men wearing nothing but a G-string, sex was something she took seriously. Sharing herself with a guy opened all sorts of vulnerabilities. She'd seen what had happened when her mother had somewhat accidentally—mostly on purpose—gotten pregnant with Lacey to keep Lacey's dad around. Hadn't worked.

On the other hand, she hoped she was smarter than her mother, and she sure wasn't looking for a last-ditch effort to sink her claws into some guy for the next eighteen-odd years.

All Keeley wanted was some temporary fun and games. Dane had successfully uprooted himself from his farm background and would probably be off like a shot once their project was completed. Kind of a built-in escape clause for the both of them.

She peeked over her shoulder, noting the breadth of his shoulders tapering to that trim waist. He was certainly the best-looking man she'd run into for a long while. Dane suddenly looked up from his computer, sensing her glance. "Do you need anything, Cherry?"

Finally, the right person was asking that question at the right time. She smiled at him. "No, not yet. But ask me later."

5

"BARBECUE?" DANE inhaled the spicy-sweet scent greedily as he found Keeley in the conference room unpacking takeout boxes. It had been months since he had had a decent barbecue dinner. "I thought we were eating those Chinese leftovers from last night." Over the past four evenings, Keeley had surprised him with Chicago deep-dish pizza, Chicago-style hot dogs with pickle spears and celery salt, huge sub sandwiches and the best Chinese food he'd tasted outside Hong Kong.

"No, I gave the leftovers to the homeless guy who sleeps outside the office building. I had a craving for a pulled pork sandwich and coleslaw." She opened a box. "And you looked like a man who likes a full slab of ribs."

"Oh, man. I love ribs and slaw." He surreptitiously patted his belly to make sure it wasn't starting to hang over his belt. He wasn't burning off four thousand calories a day doing farmwork anymore. Definitely some time on the treadmill and in the weight room downstairs was called for.

"Have a seat, then, and eat." She passed him the ribs and a cup of coleslaw.

"No, you sit. You've been arranging our dinners all week, so let me take of this." He pulled out a black leather conference chair and gestured for her to sit at the big polished wood table.

She gave him a quizzical look, as if no one had ever held out her chair for her. "Okay, Dane." She sat and smoothed her tiny red skirt over her thighs. Lucky skirt.

He distracted himself by passing her several paper napkins to protect her clothing and popped open her sandwich box. "Mmm, looks good." He grabbed a fork for her from the white plastic carryout bag.

"You can try some if you'd like." She sipped at her soft drink. "Ahh, caffeine."

"I don't want to eat your food on you. I have plenty." Instead of handing her the utensil, he sat next to her and forked a mouthful of tender, saucy meat and offered it to her. "Try yours before it gets cold."

Her green eyes widened in surprise but she opened her shiny red lips and closed them around the fork. Lucky fork. She closed her eyes and sighed as if she'd been kissed really long and really hard.

His mouth watered, and not from the barbecue aroma. He'd been fighting his attraction to her ever since he'd met her, but now he was wondering if he should have his head examined to be in a hurry to get away from this beautiful woman.

"Yum. That's even better than usual. You've gotta try it." She pulled the fork from his slack grasp and scooped up some barbecue. "Open, Dane."

Her wrist trembled a bit, so he cupped it to steady it. Her pulse was thready under his fingers, giving away her state of mind. So he wasn't the only one feeling this pull.

He forced himself to eat and managed to avoid

dropping sauce on himself. Finally, he pushed back from the table. "You really outdid yourself."

"Thanks, I almost broke a nail dialing the barbecue joint." She lifted a red-tipped finger. "It was a close call."

"No, I mean not just for the food, but for agreeing to do this, Keeley."

"Shhh." She put her finger to her lips. "Cherry, remember?"

"Cherry." He had forgotten to call her by her alias. Her nearness was making him sloppy. "I know you've gotten a lot of unwanted attention here, and you've been a real sport."

"That's me, a team player." She stood and threw away the boxes and rib bones. Wiping off her hands with a wet wipe, she turned back to him. "Although all the accounts I've looked at so far seem okay, I get a funny feeling."

"Funny, how?" The other accountants he'd come across had absolutely no intuition or imagination whatsoever.

Keeley shook her head. "I can't explain it. I think Binky's probably right about something being wrong. There's a weird vibe here in the office. It reminds me of the place where I worked while I was in school. Money was missing, and the employees were all scared of the assistant manager's nasty temper. But it wasn't him who was stealing. I hoped it was him, but it was the bookkeeper, a mousy little chick who wanted the dough for breast implants."

Dane choked on his pop, the carbonation burning the back of his throat. "She stole money for those?"

"Some women feel inadequate with small breasts."

Keeley shrugged. "I guess she wanted to learn what it was like to have backaches or loss of feeling to her nipples."

He held up his hands in not-quite-mock horror. "Whoa, whoa, too much information."

"And you a close friend of Binky's." She shook her head. "Tsk, tsk. Surely you don't think all those exotic dancers have been naturally blessed in their cup size?"

"I guess I never thought about it. I don't think I've ever dated anybody with implants, at least that I knew about," he qualified.

She gave him a skeptical look, but he was only telling her the truth. "Anyway, Dane, the point is that people will steal big money for what you and I think would be stupid reasons. My accounting professors told us, 'If you're going to steal, steal big.' The penalty for stealing fifty dollars is as bad as stealing five thousand. Each single theft is often a federal felony count and can carry up to several thousand dollars in fines and five years in prison."

Dane whistled. Several thousand in fines wouldn't bother Charlie Bingham, but hard time in the federal pen would. "Did that bookkeeper go to prison?"

Keeley made a face. "No. Turns out she was somebody's cousin, so it was all handled privately."

"But other people's money—"

She shrugged. "That job was a restaurant-type place. Lots of cash coming and going and no one was interested in opening the books for the authorities."

"Oh." That wasn't the problem at Bingham Brothers—their worry was the bad publicity and potential loss of client confidence, especially if Charlie was the bad guy. "Did you audit those books, too?"

"Yeah, in my downtime." She laughed. "This audit is

a piece of cake compared to that. No drunken customers, no earsplitting music, no puddles of beer on the floor."

"Sounds like a great place to work."

"It wasn't the best but it paid the bills and got me through school." Keeley sat in her chair and flipped open her laptop. "You said Binky had a bad feeling about the trust accounts?"

Obviously she wanted to get back to work, so Dane pointed to the accounts Binky had flagged. "See what you can find. Whatever it is, it's slipped through the safeguards here."

She arched an eyebrow at him. "Or someone here is slipping it through on their own."

"True." Dane turned to his own laptop, determined to follow Keeley's good example. Although he realized he was just playing the role of controller-in-training, Dane found himself making lists of what he would change if he actually had the job. Glenn, the real controller, had been with the company for close to thirty years and was content to do things the way they'd always been done.

On the plus side, Bingham Brothers had a firm reputation and solid financial practices, aside from the possible disastrous embezzlement. But Adam had been right. Bingham Brothers was firmly stuck in some other decade, and Dane wasn't sure which. Probably the fifties or early sixties—the financial structure was clunky and the accounting systems outdated.

He was no forensic accountant like Keeley but he had found several places where stealing from Bingham Brothers would be easier than taking candy from a baby. At least babies put up a squawk, and the Bingham accounts were silent as the grave.

Dane shook his head. He didn't blame Binky—after all, the man was in his seventies and not familiar with all the latest practices. But Charlie wasn't doing his job, either. Was it laziness or more deliberate? He didn't know.

But as long as Binky was paying him a controller's salary, Dane could be useful. Energy rushed through him. Maybe he could leave some ideas for the next real controller to implement—better accounting practices, more efficient internal reporting and accurate corporate tax planning. On the surface, it wouldn't be any different than any other consulting job.

After all, once Keeley gave him the results from the audit, he was free to leave again, maybe to Europe this time. Plenty of companies needed consulting advice on how to deal with the changing European economy.

That was what he'd wanted ever since he was a kid. No more cows, no more cow shit—just him with his well-worn passport, traveling the world.

A tapping noise startled him out of his reverie. Keeley, her eyes narrowed, stared at her computer screen, her pencil eraser beating on the desk. She looked up at him. "Sorry, Dane. It helps me think."

"Okay." The more she thought, the faster she'd finish and then it was bon voyage. Without Keeley. He frowned at that uneasy notion.

Why was Dane scowling at her? Keeley scowled back. She was going as fast as she could and her lack of progress was starting to piss her off. "If the pencil tapping bothers you, say so." Keeley wasn't interested in trying to tiptoe around some guy's bad mood. She didn't get paid to jolly men around anymore.

"No, no, it's not that. Honestly." He still looked like

someone had stolen his favorite Green Bay Packers football jersey.

"What's with the grouchy look?"

"Just thinking. Geez, cut me a break here. Does my every expression have to be analyzed?"

"Get over yourself! Like I want to know what's going on in that crabby head of yours." She glared at her computer screen. It was there, beyond her reach. *Come on, you thief. You made a mistake somewhere.*

"Keeley?" His soft voice broke her concentration yet again.

"What?" She whipped around, ready to snap at him.

"I'm sorry." He still looked grouchy, but a bit sheepish at the same time. "Listen, I know we've been putting in fourteen- or fifteen-hour days this past week, you must be beat."

"I'm fine." She turned back to her computer. He thought this job was hard. Ha! She sat on her ass all day, and the only tired part of her was her mouse finger.

His big hand came to rest on hers, stopping her mouse-clicking. She startled, and he smiled at her. "Enough."

"What's enough?"

"Look, Keeley. It's Friday night. This audit isn't some iron-man endurance test. The accounts will still be there Monday."

"You hope," she joked, but he was right. "It has been a long week."

"You mentioned you had to cancel a date earlier to work late. You still have time to call the guy and re-schedule for tonight." He examined her face closely.

"No, not tonight." He didn't need to know her date had been imaginary. Keeley slipped a pencil under her red hair and scratched her head. "I'll probably go home and take off this stupid itchy wig."

"Take it off now. I've only seen you once as a brunette."

"Dane." She frowned at him. "Anyone could come by, and then what? Explain you have a fetish for redheads and that's why I wear a wig? Don't be silly."

He shrugged. "You're right. Let's finish so you can go home and get out of those clothes."

She muffled a snicker, and he grimaced. "That didn't quite come out right."

"No, that's okay." She pushed her chair away from the table and lifted her leg to show him one torturous high heel. "I've been wearing these Lucite monstrosities for over twelve hours today. I'm going to file a complaint with occupational health and safety if I can't take them off soon." She rotated her ankle to relieve some foot pain when she caught his hungry blue stare eating up the sight of her.

"You have great legs," he rasped. "They've been driving me nuts since the coffee shop."

"Really? Even covered by my ugly brown outfit?"

"Yep." He nodded. "I could tell by the way you walked—almost like a dancer."

Keeley lowered her leg. How much to tell him? She stuck with partial truth. "I was a dancer in high school musicals and was on the pom-pom squad."

"I knew it." He gave her legs a lingering glance and shook his head as if recalling himself to professionalism. "Come on, I'll drop you off at home. On Monday, we'll pick up the audit where we left off."

Before Keeley could wallow in her disappointment, she heard a sound nearby and stood. The conference room was situated in a corner for less office noise, but there was little warning of anybody coming. "Quiet, Dane." It was probably just the cleaning crew.

Dane looked over her shoulder. "Quick, it's Charlie." Charles Andrew Bingham VI's dark head crossed a cubicle divider two rows away.

Dane began closing manila files, but Keeley had a better idea for throwing Charlie off the track. He expected the worst, so she'd give it to him.

Slamming her laptop screen shut, she hopped onto the conference table, sitting on the paperwork. "Come here." She hooked her supposedly great legs around Dane's and pulled him close, yanking his mouth to hers.

His surprised *mmmph* quickly turned into a pleased hum as he enthusiastically dove into the kiss. His lips were firm and warm as they clung greedily to hers. Keeley gave a moan and eagerly opened under his testing tongue. He dipped it into her mouth and she sucked on it eagerly. His big hands scorched her shoulder blades through her thin blouse as he settled into the cradle of her thighs. She wiggled her bottom closer, her miniskirt hiking up her thighs.

Papers hit the floor and scattered but Keeley didn't care. After all, none of them said *Charlie Bingham is a big, fat crook*.

Dane pressed hot kisses down her neck and Keeley cried out in pleased surprise as he dropped his hands, squeezing and cupping her ass. "Oh, yeah, Dane!" His erection pressed against her inner thigh.

"You like that, don't you, Kee—"

She muffled his slipup with a hard kiss, and none too soon.

"Well, well, Mr. Weiss." Charlie Bingham stood in the door, a nasty expression on his face. "My grandfather *did* teach you everything he knows. Banging the secretaries was one of his favorite pastimes as well."

Dane looked up from Keeley, his lust-softened gaze sharpening at Charlie's accusation. "Too bad your grandfather didn't teach you manners." He removed his hands from her butt but didn't step away from her. "Cherry and I were leaving. If you have anything to say to me, save it for Monday."

Charlie sputtered for a second but apparently decided not to press the issue. Keeley hopped off the table, blocking Charlie's view of Dane's erection. She tugged her skirt down and stacked files, hoping the men didn't notice her trembling hands.

"You haven't heard the end of this, Weiss. Grandpa may have gotten away with this kind of thing back in the day, but times are different now. You have five minutes to clear out before I call security." Charlie glared at them and stomped away.

"For what, Charlie? Working late on a Friday?" Dane called after him.

Keeley shook her head. "Let's go before he changes his mind. Are you sure he can't fire us?"

"Positive." Dane stuffed the papers into his case while she shut off her computer. "Binky hired me, Binky's the only one who can fire me. Chuckles knows that damn well."

"Which is why he's so ticked off. You're winning the pissing contest and he hasn't even unzipped his pants."

Dane stopped his packing and roared with laughter. "Keeley, you do have a way with words—hasn't unzipped his pants." He tapered off into an uneasy chuckle as he obviously realized the condition of his own zipper.

There was an awkward pause and they both busied themselves clearing out the conference room and getting their things.

The specter of their kiss loomed between them as they rode to the parking garage, Dane only breaking the silence long enough to ask her where she lived. He sure was one closemouthed son-of-a-gun tonight. Except when he had it open to French-kiss her.

Keeley shifted uneasily in the leather seat of his luxury sedan in a futile attempt to relieve the ache between her thighs.

Dane looked over at her once he'd pulled out of the garage into the dusky evening. "You okay?"

"Sure." No, she wasn't. Idiotic man. She guessed she'd have to spell out everything for him. "Do you think Charlie suspects me?"

"No." He stared straight ahead, the streetlights flashing over his face in a pattern that made it difficult to read his expression.

She tried again. "I don't think so, either. I mean, walking in on us with my legs wrapped around yours and your tongue in my mouth—what was he supposed to think?"

His knuckles whitened around the steering wheel and he made a choking sound.

Encouraged, Keeley continued, "And when you grabbed my ass, that was the master touch. The only way we could have been more obvious was if we were actually having sex. You know, me flat on my back on the conference table, my knees in the air while you—"

Her sentence was cut off by the brakes screeching and her seat belt locking. Dane had almost run a red light.

He swiped a hand over his face. "Geez, Keeley."

"Sorry." Sorry for almost getting them into an accident but not sorry about teasing him. "I didn't mean to embarrass you."

Turning to her, his eyes were shadowed. "I'm not embarrassed. Far from it." He started to lean over to her, but the car behind him beeped. "Shit!"

He stomped on the gas pedal, his rapid acceleration tossing her against her seat. They were coming to the on-ramp to the Kennedy expressway that would take her home, and Keeley didn't want to end the evening being dropped in front of her greystone building.

She considered inviting Dane in to her place, but quickly discarded that idea. She'd never let any man she was dating into her place and wasn't ready for Dane to be the first.

"Dane." She laid her hand on his forearm and immediately his muscles tensed. "Why don't we stop for a drink somewhere to relax?" She spotted the bar where she'd had drinks with Sugar and pointed. "They have good martinis and it's early enough that it won't be extremely crowded."

"Are you sure?" He gave her a skeptical look. "I've been working you hard all week."

"I'm a big girl. I can take it."

"I bet you can." His tone was admiring as he swerved into a nearby parking lot. "You're a real go-getter. Do you always get what you want?"

Hmm. That was a tough question. On the one hand, life hadn't given her a free pass on anything. But on the other hand, tonight she was leaving a well-paying gig in a fancy car with a sexy man she wanted to seduce. Maybe the planets were finally aligning for her. "Tonight, I think I'll get everything I want."

6

"NOT EXTREMELY crowded, huh?" Dane shouted back at her as he bulldozed a path through the mob of happy-hour revelers, triumphantly setting their drinks on the last empty table in the bar. He was actually glad to be around a bunch of people. Keeley didn't know it, but she'd barely made it out of the car without him pouncing on her.

Was that kiss in the office purely for Charlie's benefit, or had she been waiting for a chance to kiss him? It had definitely morphed into something real for him, but he couldn't tell what she thought.

Keeley shrugged and picked up her key lime martini. "I've never been here after work." Dane looked around. The place was packed with yuppies who'd obviously come straight from the office, judging from the number of suits. Most of the women had added some red lipstick and unbuttoned their jackets to reveal some slinky undergarments, but they were no competition for Keeley. She stood out among the gray and black wool like a long-legged flamingo among crows.

"No matter." Dane hoisted his martini and clinked hers on the rim. "To our project."

"To our project," she echoed, sipping the pale green drink. "Yum."

"Amazing what they call a martini these days." He shook his head and took a sip of his own. "Now *this* is a true martini."

She peered over at his drink. "What kind of martini did you get?"

"The old classic. Gin and vermouth over a couple of olives."

"Shaken or stirred?"

"Actually whipped quite soundly for being naughty."

She let out a giggle, the first genuine one he'd heard from her red lips. She occasionally laughed, but it was mostly cynical or polite laughter. "You should do that more often."

"What?" She turned her gaze back to him from where she'd been scanning the room.

"Laugh more often. Life's not that serious."

"Says the man who works eighty-hour weeks and almost starts fistfights with upper management."

She had him there. "Well, do as I say, not as I do."

"And what do you say I should do?" She lifted the slender curl of lime peel garnish from the rim of her glass and dipped it into her mouth, rotating her tongue slowly around its spiral.

Dane's mouth went dry and he sipped some of his own drink. "I say you should tell me why you kissed me." Talk about looking a gift horse in the mouth, but he wanted to know if it was solely for Charlie's benefit or if she'd wanted to kiss him.

"Ah, the conference room kiss." She stared thoughtfully at him, her hazel eyes unreadable.

"Yes, *that* kiss." And her thighs grabbing him and his hands grabbing her, but they both knew what he meant.

Just then, the lights dimmed and an obnoxious-sounding DJ blared over the crowd, cutting off Keeley's response. Apparently this bar had dancing on Friday nights.

Dane savagely crushed an olive between his teeth. Good grief, what kind of sap was he, asking a sexy woman why she'd kissed him. Next thing he knew, he'd be asking her how she felt about him and where she thought their relationship was going. Might as well call him Dana and slap a long blond wig on *his* head. He slugged back the rest of his martini. He either needed to take his chances with her or take her home.

Out of the corner of his eye, he caught her yawning. Guess that meant he should take her home. He stood so rapidly his chair skittered. "Come on, you're tired. I'll take you home."

She looked puzzled. Then the music started and she perked up her ears. Dane listened for a couple seconds. Oh, yeah, "Love Shack" by the B-52s, the national anthem for singles bars throughout America. It had originally come out when he was in middle school, back when he wouldn't have known what to do with a woman if she'd parachuted naked into his bedroom. Didn't look like much had changed.

Keeley stood and extended her hand. "Let's dance."

Dance? Oh, man. She didn't know what she was asking. He was such a bad dancer his sister-in-law had actually badgered him into taking lessons before her wedding to his brother. The lessons hadn't worked.

But to keep Keeley near him for even a while longer, he'd dance the cha-cha slide. Or even that "YMCA" song. "Um, okay." He took her hand, followed her to the tiny dance floor and took a deep breath. Here goes nothin'.

She smiled at him, her high heels bringing her to almost eye-level with him. He'd never danced with such a tall girl before, but realized it wasn't a bad idea. At least he didn't have to worry about crushing her underfoot.

"Relax, Dane," she shouted over the B-52s whooping it up.

He gave her what he thought was a relaxed smile, but she giggled again.

"Okay, I'll show you." And with that, it was as if she'd flipped that sex-kitten switch. She rolled her hips bonelessly, her shoulders moving in the same rhythm. He didn't even try to dance, just stood in awe. Her eyes were closed in pleasure as she sang along with the music. She didn't just move like a dancer, she really *was* one.

She opened her eyes to see him standing there like a dumbass. "Come on!" she urged him. "Try!"

He tried his best to move, but it was hopeless. Her full breasts jiggling under her tiny top and the curves of her ass under that micro-miniskirt kept distracting him…and every other guy within twenty feet. When he wasn't watching Keeley, he was throwing nasty looks at the more blatant starers.

The song ended and moved into another hard-thumping dance tune. "Vogue" by Madonna? Boy, this DJ was in a time warp, but Keeley obviously didn't care as she spun into a series of dazzling turns. Dane didn't know beans about dancing, but she sure knew her moves. That downstate high-school pom-pom squad must have been glad to have her.

He could tell she really enjoyed dancing. Her face was tilted upward in what could only be called a joyful expression, a wide grin cutting across her face.

When had Dane last felt anything close to pure joy? Probably when his nieces and nephew were born, but aside from that? Sad to say, he couldn't remember.

Madonna's last "vogue" faded away and Keeley clapped and cheered, perspiration making her skin glisten like gold under the lights. When one stray drop trailed its way between her breasts, Dane's last itsy-bitsy vestige of control snapped and he pulled her close.

Her body fit perfectly against him, heat radiating between the two of them that he didn't think was entirely the result of her exertions. He cupped the nape of her neck with his hand, the rough edge of her wig fueling his resolve to see her pretty brown hair again.

She looked at him and licked her lips. That was all the invitation he needed. He dove onto her mouth and she eagerly opened under him, all sweet-and-sour from her drink. He nibbled on her lower lip and ran his tongue along her ridge of white teeth. He imagined those lips and teeth rasping along his body and groaned. She moaned in return, resting her hands on his chest right above his thundering heart.

Dane had been half-afraid to kiss her in the worry that the kiss in the office had been for show. But here on the crowded dance floor, Keeley responded with as much eagerness, as much sweetness. He kissed her soft cheek, her firm jaw and the tender skin behind her ear. She clutched at his lapels, her breath hot on his face.

Someone jostled Keeley, breaking their embrace. Dane reluctantly lifted his mouth from the smooth column of her neck. Breathing hard, Keeley rested her forehead on his shoulder as another dance tune started.

Dane needed to get her out of the bar and somewhere private. The music was drilling through his brain and his cock was trying to drill through his pants.

Keeley refused to meet his gaze, trying to get them back to the dance lesson. "Loosen those hips and you'll do fine." She actually grabbed his hips and tried rocking them back and forth.

He put his hands over her wrists and leaned down. "If you don't stop grabbing my ass in public, I won't be responsible for the consequences." He purposefully rotated his pelvis into hers so she could feel what she'd done to him, his erection nestling against her belly.

Her eyes widened and she paused for a second. "Maybe you need a private dance lesson."

Was she offering what he thought? "I have music at my place." He waited anxiously for her response.

A smile curved her lips. "All right, let's go."

He fought back a whoop of delight. He might be a klutz when it came to dance moves, but there were other moves he did *extremely* well.

"GOOD THING WE have a parking garage under the building, huh?" Dane guided Keeley to the lobby elevator and nodded at the night doorman in his silver-trimmed navy-blue uniform.

She nodded and tried to ignore the butterflies dancing around in her stomach and concentrate on her surroundings for distraction. The whole lobby was designed with lots of stainless steel and glass with sofas in varying shades of blue.

Keeley had never been in Lakenheath Towers, not knowing anyone but Binky who could afford the place. Binky must really value Dane to house him here. Covered parking was probably the least of the amenities.

Thunder boomed outside the glass doors. She looked back. "I can't believe how fast that storm blew in." It had started right after they left the club, forcing her to let Dane concentrate on his driving. No more innuendos— Keeley wanted to spend the night with Dane, not the local E.R. staff.

The elevator arrived and the doorman called after them to have a good evening. He needn't have been concerned about that. Dane pressed the button for the sixty-third floor and Keeley watched the numbers count as they climbed.

Another huge crack of thunder reached their ears and the lights went out, the elevator skidding to a stop. Keeley stumbled, but Dane caught her before she fell. "You all right?"

"Sure, fine." Not really. She hated dark, enclosed spaces.

The emergency phone rang and Dane fumbled with the little compartment door. "Hello?" He listened for a few seconds. "Yes, we're okay. What happened?"

Keeley stood frozen in her square foot of elevator carpet.

Dane finally hung up and reached for her, finding her shoulder. "There you are. The doorman says the building lost power but the elevator's emergency brakes kicked in. We should be on our way in a few minutes."

"Okay." She hated how small and frightened her voice was, but couldn't help it.

Dane gathered her into his arms. "Don't be scared. We'll be fine." He kissed her on the forehead, just like he probably kissed his sister.

Keeley couldn't help the tears that began to flow. It figured. The first man she'd wanted to seduce in months, if not years, and here she was stuck in a small dark place too petrified to even move.

He heard her sniffle. "Oh, hey, no crying." He rubbed his hands over her back, and brushed his lips over one wet cheek, then the next. "Don't cry, sweetheart. I'm here. I'll take care of you."

Keeley stopped crying, shocked by his words. She couldn't remember the last time anyone had taken care of her. Not her mother, never her father, and her sister had been too young.

Dane misunderstood her silence. "There, that's better. As soon as the elevator starts, I'll take you home. Promise."

What a sweet man. Her desire for him roared back, multiplied by his tender concern. She unclenched her fists and wrapped her arms around his neck.

"Thank you, Dane." And she kissed him. Not like the quick, urgent kiss for Charlie's benefit, but a slow, tender kiss where their lips clung and parted several times, learning each other's taste and scent. He had wonderful lips, smooth and warm, his stubble sensitizing her mouth until she could feel every dip and curve of his.

He seemed content to let her explore his mouth, following her lead. His breathing sped, but he had lots of patience.

He thumbed the nape of her neck. "Let's get this wig off, Keeley. I want to know how your soft, wavy hair feels under my hands."

"Probably not so great. It's been pinned up all day."

"Don't care." He nibbled at her ear. "It's you. It's real."

The real her. Despite his brave words, she didn't think he was ready for that. But she'd wanted to take off the wig since lunchtime. She loosened the mesh cap and lifted it off, setting it carefully on her laptop case on the floor.

He felt his way around, pulling out her hairpins and massaging her scalp with his long, strong fingers.

She whimpered with pleasure and rolled her neck. "Oh, that feels good."

"I want to make you feel good." He ran his hands through her hair and cupped her head. She was in a very vulnerable position, but with him, she didn't mind. In fact, she even went on tiptoe and gave him a soft kiss.

"Smile for me," she whispered against his lips.

"You can't see it in the dark, Keeley," he whispered, obviously not wanting to wreck their intimacy, either.

"Please, sweetheart."

His arms tightened around her. "I smiled as soon as you called me that."

Sure enough, his mouth had widened under hers. She took her chance and dipped her tongue into both deep dimples bracketing his cheeks.

"Whatcha doing?" His tone was indulgent.

"You have the cutest dimples. I've wanted to stick my tongue in them ever since we met at the coffee shop."

He groaned and carefully eased his hips away from her. "Keeley, if you keep talking like that, I'm not going to take you home."

She closed the gap between him and backed him against the wall, her breasts pushing into his chest. "Maybe I don't want you to take me home. Maybe I want you to take me here." She held her breath. She'd never been so blunt with a man, but Dane seemed to be a guy who responded best to bluntness.

He didn't say a word; instead he kissed her again. This time their kisses were fast and hot as he trailed his lips over her neck, nipping and sucking at her sensitive skin. She quickly unbuttoned her blouse and urged his head downward, glad she'd worn her supersheer microfiber bra today. Since they were in the dark, touch was everything.

He eagerly complied, brushing his face over her breasts in the silky fabric. "So nice and soft."

"My best bra."

He chuckled. "Not the bra—what's in it." He cupped her breasts with his big hands. "Wonderful." His thumbs traced lazy patterns over her nipples, tightening them unbearably. She tottered on her high heels a bit and he spun her around so her back rested in the cold mirrored wall.

"Tell me one thing, baby." His tone was husky and intimate.

"Anything." She was falling under his seductive spell now. A broken claustrophobic elevator was turning out to be the best thing ever.

"Tell me what color your nipples are." He pinched them and she gave a little gasp. "I'm about to suck on them and I want to imagine their color as they harden and swell in my mouth."

She shuddered. His erotic-book-narrator tone was back, making her hips twitch against his.

He removed his hands. "I won't suck you unless you tell me."

Anything but that. "Um." She thought frantically if fuzzily. She'd certainly seen enough of them over the

years and under stage lights, too. What color were they?
"Oh! Light brown."

"Very good." He put his hands on her and she sighed
with relief and anticipation. He popped the front clasp
to her bra and her breasts swung free, but not for long.
Dane took one in each hand and groaned. "Just like I
thought—you have the smoothest skin."

"You're sweet," she whispered.

"No, *you're* sweet." He rolled her nipples between
his fingers. "I was hard for you in the coffee shop and
to have you in my office every day with these sexy
blouses. Do you know how many times you asked me
to look over your shoulder at the computer and all I
wanted to do was slide my hands under your shirt?"

"I wanted you to," she confessed, panting slightly as
his grip tightened.

"And there are a lot of things I want to do to you,"
he promised. He kept his promise and sucked a nipple
into his mouth. She tightened her fingers in his hair,
barely keeping her balance as he swept his tongue
around her in a lazy pattern.

First one nipple, and then the other, he moved back
and forth, curving his free hand around her ass.

He dropped to his knees, his hot breath level with her
belly button. Keeley groaned.

"Ah, I'd love to eat you right now, but I want to be
able to take my time when I lick your sweet pussy."
Instead, he put one hand on each of her ankles and
slowly slid his palms upward, massaging her calves and
shins, tickling the back of her knees until she giggled.

He moved up the backs of her thighs and she quickly
got serious. He eased his hands under her stretchy mini-

skirt and gently snapped her thong strap. "A dancer's ass in a thong." His big hands cupped her bare bottom. "I can die happy now."

"You better not." She deliberately rolled her hips in her best stripper mode ever, since it was sincere and not pretend. "I intend on both of us being a *lot* happier in the next few minutes." She urged him to his feet. "Now, Dane."

"But I haven't touched you that much."

"I haven't touched you, either, but I think we're more than ready." She dragged his hand to the front of her panties where they both felt her moisture. "Now, Dane," she repeated.

She heard the clink of his belt and rustling clothing. He turned away from her and fumbled in his bag for protection, which he quickly donned. Keeley yanked her stretchy skirt around her waist and stripped off her thong.

He pressed her into the wall again and groaned, his erection massive on her belly. "Keeley, our first time should be somewhere nice. You deserve everything good."

She cupped his face in her hands, running her thumbs over his cheeks. No dimples—he must be serious. "I deserve *you*, and I want our first time to be right now. Besides, if I could actually *see* that monster cock of yours coming at me, I might scream and run away."

He choked out a laugh. "You're wicked. I like wicked women."

He had no idea. "Good." She gripped his erection and guided it to her pulsing clit. She rubbed his tip over her, causing him to jerk in her hand.

He braced his hands on the wall on either side of her shoulders and dropped his head, breathing heavily. "Okay, Keeley. I can't wait any longer."

Slowly, she shifted her hips so he prodded her gently and stopped when she tensed. It had been a long time for her, and he was much larger than she had expected.

"Relax, baby." He nuzzled her hair, his breath hot in her ear. "You're so hot and slick, I can slide right in."

She closed her eyes and let go of the fearful tension, keeping only the lovely sensual pressure. He inched in, filling and stretching her, stopping every few seconds to make sure she was okay.

Keeley couldn't stand the gradual pace anymore and hooked her leg around his, pulling him in to the hilt. They both cried out as he throbbed inside her, her face buried in the crook of his neck, his resting on her hair.

"Perfect," he whispered. "You're the perfect size for me."

She had never been so completely filled, her pussy clenching around him. He gave a little gasp. "Do that again." She complied, squeezing him with every single muscle she could.

"Yesss," he hissed, beginning to pump in and out of her, the base of his shaft hitting her clit with every stroke. She thrust back at him, meeting him stroke for stroke.

"Ah, we're perfect together…the right height to fuck standing, especially with those crazy shoes." Dane was turning out to be a sex-talker, and Keeley loved it, his stream of words making her even hotter.

"More," she commanded when he stopped talking.

"More of this?" He sped his thrusting. "Or this?" His big finger brushed her clit.

"Yes! And talk dirty to me."

His low chuckle rumbled through her. "I don't know if I can. You've had me hard as a rock, and now that we're finally together, all I can think of is making you scream my name."

"Dane," she moaned.

He rubbed her clit faster, his broad chest heaving as well. "Louder." He thumbed her nipple with his other hand. "So soft and sweet. I want to see you in my bed wearing nothing but those shoes."

She shuddered as his hips jolted into hers. "Then what?"

"Then I'm gonna spread those sexy legs of yours wide open and see if your pussy tastes as great as it feels."

The image of her naked under his mouth made her moan. She bet he would tend to her with all the detail he showed with everything else.

"You're close, aren't you? Please, tell me you're close."

Unable to speak, Keeley nodded into his shoulder.

"Hold on, baby." He let go of her breast and braced himself on the elevator wall.

Keeley couldn't hold back a cry as he charged into her, his big head hitting all the juicy spots deep inside her. They were making the elevator shake, but she didn't care. Dane was with her, inside her, around her, and he would keep her safe.

His finger pressed her clit one last time and his name burst from her lips in a scream, just as he'd promised. She pulsed around his cock, the shock waves rushing into her belly, breaking over her breasts until she thought she'd drop to the floor. She tossed her head back, greedily inhaling how his sexy musky scent mixed with her own. If the elevator plunged to the basement, at least she'd go with a smile.

But Dane had other ideas. He moved his other hand

to the wall. "Put your legs around my waist and hold on," he groaned.

She complied, too drained to protest. He took her full weight without flinching. She really had to get a look at those muscles of his. She was no skinny-mini.

Now that he wasn't holding back to wait for her, he really let her have it, his heavy, tight balls slapping her bottom as he pistoned in and out. "Ah, Keeley, so sexy, so sweet, so tight," he chanted.

His sex talk, combined with his rapid thrusting, was making her hot again. Her every sense was heightened, the warm musky smell of their lovemaking, the heat of his body, the sound of his voice. She rotated her hips against him as if she were doing a lap dance, her clit bumping his shaft.

"So wicked." He was starting to gasp now, close to his own orgasm. "Making me hard, waking up hard, that ass, those tits." He groaned as Keeley licked the salty column of his neck, his cock swelling even fatter inside her. "Dying to see you…"

She was dying to see him, too, dying to see his face as he came, dying to see the rod that was giving her such pleasure. Keeley trembled as another orgasm pulsed through her, her nails digging into his rock-hard shoulders as she arched away from him. Dane bellowed her name and erupted, his hips pounding into hers until the elevator shook again. His climax lasted forever, jolting her pussy with aftershocks. She rested her face on his shoulder, shaken by their lovemaking's intensity.

Finally, he stilled, his breath still fast and rasping. He nuzzled her face until he found her lips. She kissed him back, a kiss that was surprisingly innocent, considering he was locked hard inside her.

The elevator bounced and Dane wrapped his arms around her. Keeley gasped.

"It's okay. They'll probably get us moving soon." Dane kissed her forehead. "But we should probably dress. I can't exactly carry you to my condo sitting naked on top of me."

"Why not?" She deliberately squeezed him.

He retaliated by giving her a light smack on the ass. "Because nobody sees you naked but me. Hell, I haven't even seen you naked yet."

Keeley flinched and relaxed. Water under the bridge. It wasn't as if she planned an encore performance at the Love Shack anytime soon. "Same goes for you."

"Deal." He kissed her forehead and eased her legs to the floor, helping her regain her shaky balance.

A few moments later, Keeley had made herself as presentable as possible but decided to forego the wig. The lights in the elevator turned on and she caught a glimpse of herself, sweaty and disheveled, her hair sticking up in clumps where the pins had come free. "Ugh."

"What?" Dane, on the other hand, looked as if he'd just taken off his tie after a long day at the office.

"What will the neighbors think?"

Dane grinned. "They'll think I'm the luckiest SOB in Chicago."

7

DANE DIDN'T BOTHER offering Keeley a grand tour of his condo. He set her laptop and wig on a foyer table and scooped up her not-unsubstantial person.

"Don't hurt yourself, Dane. I'm not one of those petite blondes you claim to prefer."

He grinned at her as he carried her down a marble-tiled hallway. "I thought that might get you. I actually love brunettes." He ran his tongue along her ear. "Tall, sexy brunettes who dance for me and take me standing in an elevator."

She shuddered and slipped her hand inside his open collar. His chest was hard and warm, bunching as he balanced her weight easily. She was glad he had started to seduce her again. Things were less awkward if they could delay or even avoid the now-that-we've-had-crazy-elevator-sex-where-do-we-go-from-here? conversation.

The only place Dane was going was the bedroom, apparently. He shouldered open the door to the dark room and dropped her on the bed, where she landed in a poof of slippery bedding. She heard his fast breathing and the rustle of his clothing. "Dane, turn the light on."

He groaned. "I'm not sure that's a good idea?"

"Why? Do you have a weird tattoo?" Or maybe a

birthmark or a scar. "Never mind—we can leave the light off."

"No weird tattoos." He sounded amused. "It's this bedroom—a major mood killer."

"Seeing you will more than make up for it."

"You may want to reserve judgment." His shadow crossed the rectangle of light from the door and the room was illuminated in all its froufrou glory.

"Wow." Keeley blinked at the six-foot-wide crystal-and-gold teardrop chandelier in the center of the room. The bed where she lay was an elaborate four-postered white frame complete with gilding all around. The bedding was real gold silk, complete with several tasseled and embroidered gold-and-white pillows. A matching gold-upholstered divan sat in the corner along with a pair of spindly gold-and-white chairs. Pink floor-length curtains and a large pink rug added a dash of color.

"Yeah. Wow," Dane said sourly, crossing his arms over his unbuttoned shirt. "I swear that I had nothing to do with this monstrosity. Binky said his interior designer planned this as a lady's elegant boudoir."

Keeley tried to muffle her giggles but they came out as a loud snort. "Boudoir—I feel like a mistress to a French king."

"Yeah, all it needs is a harpsichord in the corner and we'd be in Versailles." Dane stopped glaring at the pink curtains and focused on her. "On the other hand, this chandelier does throw off about five hundred watts—plenty to see each other *very* well." He slowly pulled off his shirt.

Keeley's mouth went dry. Dane had a typical

farmer's tan—his chest was pale in comparison to his arms and neck—but my, oh, my, he was built. A lifetime of tossing hay and herding cows had given him muscles on top of muscles. His broad chest was covered in golden hair, and his wide ribs tapered into a flat stomach and compact waist.

He undid his belt buckle and slowly slid it free from the loops. The stray thought passed her mind that he was performing an excellent striptease for an amateur.

Then he dropped his pants and Keeley immediately gave him professional status. Good thing he had such brawny thighs and calves to support his huge cock. She was amazed they'd fit so well together their first time—and in an elevator, no less. He was already aroused again, his erection pointing to his belly button. She licked her dry lips.

He swallowed hard and his cock jerked, a silver bead appearing on the tip. "You like what you see?"

"Oh, yeah." She couldn't take her eyes off him and pressed her thighs together to ease the throbbing between them.

"Keeley, honey," he rasped. "Take off your clothes."

"Oh." She'd been so caught up in him, she'd forgotten. Fortunately, she didn't have much to take off. She made quick work of her shirt and bra, kicking off her skirt until it got tangled on her heels.

He strode toward her and pulled the fabric free so all she wore was her shoes. She was sitting on the foot of the bed. "Lie back," he commanded. She complied, eager to have him again. He unstrapped her shoes and rested her feet on his thighs. Lifting one foot, he massaged the arch. Keeley moaned at the unexpected pleasure.

"You've had a long day on those poor feet of yours and then going out dancing. Having wild sex with me in the elevator." He moved to the ball of her foot, his strong fingers hitting every nerve ending possible.

She moved restlessly on the duvet. With one foot in the air, she couldn't ease her mounting desire.

His husky voice continued, "Don't worry, baby. I don't intend for either of us to leave this bed for a very long time. We may not even make it in to the office on Monday." He moved to her other foot. "This weekend I'll make it up to you." He swept his hand up her calf. "Every inch of your sexy golden body will feel my attention."

She couldn't stand it anymore and caressed herself, rubbing a hand over her belly and her breasts. "Such soft skin," he murmured, kissing the hollow behind her knee. She jerked in arousal. "Such pretty breasts, so full and round." He nibbled his way up her thigh. "You didn't tell me the truth, though."

"What?" She tipped her head to look at him, kneeling between her thighs, his blond hair a halo under the bright crystal chandelier. "Truth about what?" Had he learned about her past? Surely not, since he was licking his way up her legs.

"Your nipples. They're not brown—they're caramel, sweet like the rest of you, and I'm going to eat you up." He dropped his mouth to her clit and she screamed in delight.

Keeley had never been pleasured like this before. Dane worked her like a hard candy, licking and sucking as if she were the best treat ever. Tremors spread from his mouth into her belly, her breasts, her throat, making her breath squeeze and catch at his touch. He was really into her, making little hums of satisfaction. His blond stubble prickled her already sensitized inner parts.

He slid his big hands under her ass and lifted her more fully into his mouth, his tongue darting into her pussy as he rubbed his nose over her clit. She clamped her dancer's thighs around his face and heard a muffled chuckle.

He lifted his face for a second. "I'm gonna make you scream my name." He dove back and pressed one thick thumb inside her pussy and the other against her bottom, all the while his mouth working its magic on her clit. He gave one big shimmy with his tongue and Keeley exploded, her back pulling into a tight bow off the bed as he continued to pleasure her. She screamed his name loud enough to rattle the chandelier, but he clamped her to his mouth and his hands until she was hoarse.

She finally slumped into the bed as he straightened and pulled on a condom. She wondered vaguely where he got ones that fit. He parted her legs and positioned himself between them, his face red with exertion and lust. Without saying anything for once, he slid into her and they both groaned when he hit home.

"Did that hurt?" he asked anxiously.

"Not at all." She gave him what must have been a very feline smile and wrapped her legs around his waist. "Go on, Mr. Weiss. I'm very happy to take your dick— Oops, dictation."

"You are so bad, Keeley. I knew you were teasing me." He sped his thrusts a bit. "I wanted you since we met. Dreaming of you. Hot, hard, nasty dreams."

"Nasty?" Keeley shuddered in pleasure. His thick

cock was rubbing her G-spot inside. She heard of being able to come with only intercourse stimulation but hadn't done it before. If anyone could do it for her, it was Dane.

"Really nasty. Like you're a stripper and dancing for me." He grimaced in pleasure as she flinched and inadvertently squeezed him. "Like we're at the office and you suck me off behind my desk." He dipped his head and bit her earlobe.

Keeley groaned and dug her fingers into his ass. "What else?" Having sex with Dane came complete with its own soundtrack and narration. It was like being the star of her own sexy movie.

"I take you into my private office bathroom and fuck you on the sink."

"Monday."

"What?" He lifted his head in sexy confusion.

"Ten o'clock, Monday. Instead of a coffee break, we'll have a fucking break."

He gave a moan. "Really? You'd let me do that to you in the office?"

She adopted Cherry's slightly breathless voice. "I'd let you do anything to me, Mr. Weiss."

"Hey." He stopped thrusting, much to her displeasure. She wiggled a little to get him going again. "Keeley. Look at me."

She opened her eyes at his stern tone and he stared at her, a serious expression on his handsome face. "Let's make this clear—Dane Weiss is making love to Keeley Davis, not Cherry Whoever-she-is. Here, at the office— wherever. Right?"

"Right." Her eyes slammed shut so he couldn't see their sudden dampness. She opened her eyes again and tried to lighten the mood. "But I *so* wanted to pretend I was in bed with a lusty farmhand."

He roared with laughter and moved gently inside her again. "Sorry, baby. That's no fantasy—that's who I am in real life. Except we'd be upstairs in the barn on a pile of hay."

"Why, Dane, it sounds as if you've done that before." Him moving over her in a big cushy bed of hay, not wanting to get caught...for one crazy second, she almost invited herself to Wisconsin so she could screw him silly in a barn.

"I plead the Fifth, honey."

She lifted her hip and cupped his balls with one hand. "Ve haf vays of making you talk." She stroked him gently, and his sac tightened.

"Ohhh...I'll say anything you want." He lifted one of her legs to rest on his shoulder and plunged deep. "You like that?"

She nodded, groaning as the base of his shaft hit her clit over and over again. He braced himself over her body, moving with the same ferocity and determination that she'd seen at the office protecting her from Charlie.

Her climax spun and coiled until it broke her wide open and she fell apart under him. Four climaxes in such a short time was a record for her. Dane was rapidly approaching his own climax, his balls taut and hot in her hand. He let go in the same second and burst into her, pulsing. "Keeley, oh, Keeley," he continued shouting her name several times in a sex-roughened voice. She'd never heard it sound so wonderful.

He collapsed on her in a puff of silk comforter. For a couple minutes, the only sound was their noisy breathing. His weight was heavy but comforting, as if nothing bad could ever get past him.

Finally Dane rolled onto his back, taking her with him, his erection still hot inside her. She relaxed on his chest, playing with the golden-blond whorls of hair. He kissed the top of her head. "Keeley?" His tone was studiedly casual. "Did you really have a date tonight?"

She lifted her head and smiled at him. So, superconfident Dane wasn't so self-assured when it came to her. That was good. She wasn't a sure thing anymore. "And risk having to explain my red wig? No, thanks."

"I don't mean as Cherry. As Keeley, you're even more beautiful." He skimmed a hand across her cheek.

Amazingly, she felt herself blush. She hadn't blushed in years. "Well, I was too busy to date during tax season and too tired after it."

"God bless the IRS," he said fervently.

She giggled. "I wouldn't go that far."

"How far *will* you go?" He leered at her and tickled her stomach.

She sat up on his body and grabbed two handfuls of hard pecs, rubbing her thumbs over his brown nipples. He groaned and thrust into her and she rotated her hips on him. "As far as you want and further than you can imagine."

8

DANE WALKED DOWN the office hallway Monday morning, humming under his breath. He realized it was Aerosmith's "Love in an Elevator" and grinned. Thank goodness for Midwestern thunderstorms.

He passed by Charlie's office and waved cheerfully at Mrs. Hobson, the secretary who'd been at Bingham Brothers for at least thirty years. She beckoned him in, and he complied. "What can I do for you today?"

She looked over her shoulder at Charlie's inner office. "Mr. Bingham wants to see you as soon as possible."

Dane narrowed his eyes. Probably to tear him a new one about making out with Keeley in the office. He smiled reassuringly at the older lady and walked past her into the inner office. "What's up, Charlie?"

Binky's grandson looked up from his paperwork. "Close the door, Weiss."

Dane shut it, knowing the secretary would overhear their sure-to-be-loud discussion anyway. He sat in the visitor's chair across the desk with a neutral expression on his face.

Charlie shot to his feet and waggled his finger at Dane. "You are playing with fire and I don't intend to see Bingham Brothers get burned in the process."

Binky's grandson should have majored in theatre in college instead of business administration, given his overblown dramatics. He continued, "You don't see me messing with my secretary, do you?"

Dane was hard-pressed not to guffaw. Although Mrs. Hobson was well-preserved for her age and carefully dyed her hair strawberry-blond, she was old enough to be Charlie's mother.

Charlie realized the stupidity of what he said and turned even redder. "You know what I mean!" He paced back and forth across the plush Turkish carpet that had probably been unrolled by minions of the first Charles Andrew Bingham. "You are opening this firm to all sorts of problems when you get sexually involved with subordinates."

"I don't consider her my subordinate at all," he said immediately. It was true. If anything, Keeley was too good for him.

Charlie ticked off his arguments on his fingers. "Complaints to human resources, filings with the Equal Employment Opportunity Commission, civil lawsuits. Hundreds of millions of dollars have been awarded to plaintiffs in sexual harassment suits—do you want to see Bingham Brothers bankrupted?"

Dane sighed. His nemesis was correct, for once. "Of course not. But I swear it won't cause a problem for the company." Keeley wasn't technically an employee, being privately contracted by Binky. "If it makes you feel better, that episode in the conference room on Friday was a onetime thing. You don't have to worry about catching me messing with her."

"But you are seeing her outside work." It was a statement, not a question.

Dane shrugged. Even if he lied and denied it, Charlie wouldn't believe him. "We're both single adults."

Charlie exploded and slapped the desk. "Dammit, Weiss! She's the type of slutty gold digger that would string you along and then string us out to dry."

Dane leaped to his feet and slammed his fists down as well, his face about six inches from Charlie's angry one. "If you ever call Kee—Cherry that again, I will beat the crap out of you. Right here in the office." Charlie sputtered, but Dane held firm. "You know I'll do it, and your grandfather will back me up. He knows how disrespectful you are to women." Dane straightened and walked out.

Charlie stomped after him and stood next to Mrs. Hobson's desk, still spitting mad. "Mark my words, Weiss—the ones who will sleep with their bosses will do just about anything to come out on top."

Dane looked over his shoulder and shook his head. Several other staff members had witnessed Charlie's last words, including his own secretary. Mrs. Hobson sat frozen, her face pale and her mouth compressed into a tight line. Dane mouthed an apology, sorry he and Charlie had drawn her into their ugliness.

They had drawn in Keeley as well, since the office gossip would fly about her. Her assessment of their male acrimony as a pissing contest had been right on the mark. Dane was afraid he and Charlie had both peed on their shoes during this one.

KEELEY'S GLANCE kept straying away from her open files and to the computer clock. She'd promised Dane a special treat at ten o'clock Monday, but wasn't sure he'd take her up on it at the office. She hadn't seen him yet this morning since he'd had meetings scheduled.

Nine-forty-five. Even her work couldn't keep her mind off him.

Spreadsheets. His strong body spread on the fine Egyptian cotton sheets at his condo.

Calculations. How many times had he made her come as opposed to his own climaxes? A ratio of two-to-one, at least.

Numbers. How many times would they make love before they were finished with their project? Or finished with each other, more likely.

Dane strode into the office. "Hello, Miss Smith." He brushed past her into his own office and closed the door.

Well. Looked like Dane had some Monday morning regrets. It figured. She stared at the computer screen, the numbers blurring a bit. She didn't dare cry, not only for her own self-respect but because her eyelash glue and mascara would flood her cheeks.

"Cherry?" His voice came over the intercom.

"What is it, Mr. Weiss?"

"Please come in here. I need to talk to you."

Rats. She closed her audit software and blinked a couple times before joining him. "Yes?"

"We need to talk, Cherry." He sat behind his big desk, his tone as businesslike as it could be.

She grudgingly did as he asked and walked to stand next to him. "If you're going to break things off, at least have the decency to do it outside this office."

"What?" He looked startled. "Break things off?"

"That's why you're acting funny, why you called me in here, isn't it?" She gave him a cool look.

"After the weekend we had?" He narrowed his eyes. "*You* want to call it quits, don't you?"

"No. I thought you did, walking in like you did."

"Oh, that." He leaned back in his chair and gave her a serious look, devoid of any laughter they'd shared over the past three days. "I had a nasty meeting with Charlie, and I don't want to expose you to any more gossip than you already are."

"Is that all?" she scoffed, relieved. She'd been on the receiving end of more gossip than he could imagine. She smiled. He was trying to protect her reputation.

He frowned, probably at her levity. "Of course not. I thought us dating would be a good cover for our activities, but it's causing you unpleasantness. From now on, nothing but professional detachment here at Bingham Brothers."

She traced a finger over the lapel of his charcoal jacket. "We need to stick with the original plan. If people don't think I'm sleeping with you, they might start to wonder what I *am* doing here."

"Keeley," he whispered. "You should know I hired you for your qualifications, not because you were the sexiest woman I've ever met, though you are. I would have asked you out when the audit was over, but when I kissed you Friday…"

"*I* kissed *you.* And not just because Charlie was there. I wanted you, Dane. A whole lot." She stroked his red silk tie up and down. "I showed you all weekend how much I wanted you, and I still want you. Here and now."

The ornate clock on the wall chimed ten. They both

looked at it. Keeley said, "It's that time. Are you going to make me break my promise?"

Dane caught her slender wrist gently, sure she could feel his heart pounding under her hand. She was a temptress, reminding him of her sexy promise. "I can wait," he said bravely. Just being close to her was making him crazy.

"I know you can, but do you want to?" She leaned down, her low-cut top showing him firm breasts encased in black lace. "Have you ever done it at work?"

He couldn't take his eyes off her breasts. "No." Work was work, and fun was fun. He didn't mix the two. Until now.

Keeley straightened and turned, focusing his attention on her curvy ass. Now that he knew what she looked like naked, he was a goner at work. He'd need lead-lined underwear to keep from being humiliated by his permanent boner.

She gave him a sly smile. "I'll be in your private bathroom freshening up." She sauntered away and left the door ajar. Dane spun his chair and hurried after her.

She was already leaning against the granite countertop and deliberately looked at his zipper. "That didn't take long."

He closed and locked the door behind him. "You knew it wouldn't. Now what are you going to do about it?"

"This." Without warning, she dropped to her knees in front of him and reached for his belt buckle.

"You don't have to do this." He caught her shoulders but she ignored him and unfastened his pants, exposing his navy silk boxers. His dick strained against the fabric, almost jumping free in its eagerness to reach her.

"Dane, just stand there and let me do the work. No

touching." Her glossy red lips puckered and she kissed the tip of his shaft through the silk.

Her delicate touch nearly collapsed his knees and he braced himself on the sink. "Oh, Keeley…" He was startled to hear the hoarse neediness in his voice. Dane Weiss, well-known business hard-ass, was reduced to a weak-kneed wuss. Somehow, over their long sex-packed weekend, she had never put her mouth on him. Probably because he was too busy taking her from above, below and behind.

She rubbed her cheek over his cock like a kitten being petted. Her hot breath feathered through the fabric. "I love silk on a hard man. I bet a big man like you needs the extra room in boxers."

She gently spread open the front of his shorts and coaxed his penis through. The cool office air hit his overheated flesh, and he hissed out a breath.

He stared at her, the sight of his dick sticking from his business suit decidedly strange. For a second, it was as if he had a different woman with him, and his erection flagged for a moment, with Keeley wearing her red wig and overdone makeup and clothes.

But then she looked up with her rapt stare and plump lips, erasing his sense of disconnect. She sat back on her heels. "You are so sexy, Dane, dressed in that thousand-dollar Italian suit, gold cuff links and red silk tie, the epitome of male business power. And now, with your hard cock showing your sexual power." She shivered in arousal, her pupils starting to dilate, leaving only a green rim.

He hooked his hands under her arms, intending to set her on the sink and pound into her, not caring at this point if the whole office heard them. "Come here, baby, and let me show you my power."

She enfolded her red lips around him and all his so-called power went down the drain. Her hot mouth moved slowly up and down, as she wrapped her hand around the base where her mouth didn't reach.

She slid her other hand under his balls, cupping and squeezing them.

"You like playing with me, sweetheart?" She nodded, her grip tightening slightly. He sighed in contentment, knowing this was arousing her almost as much as him. "I like it, too. Did you like my balls slapping on you when we were fucking?"

She gave a little breathy moan, the vibrations fluttering along his length. He gripped the countertop for dear life, but she stopped and lifted her mouth from him. He almost cried in disappointment.

Keeley glared at him. "Stop talking, Dane. You're not in charge now."

"In charge?"

"You know what I mean. All that sex talk makes me crazy for you."

"It does?" He started to grin. She must have not liked that since she gripped his balls a bit tighter. "Sorry. I won't do it anymore."

"This is for you, all for you." She darted out her pink tongue and licked a bead off the slit. "Mmm. Wonder what more would taste like?" He shuddered in desire, making more fluid coat his tip. "Yum, looks like I'll find out." She spiraled her tongue around his blood-purpled head.

"Please, baby, suck me. I'll do anything you want," he begged her. Begged her? He never begged women to do anything. They were eager to please *him*. But she sucked his cock hard into her hot wet mouth and he begged his little heart out. "Oh, don't stop."

She didn't, working him with her lips, tongue and even teeth as she let him know who was boss now. His hips thrust helplessly as she controlled his rhythm, controlled his arousal. His entire world shrunk to his throbbing erection slipping in and out of her tempting mouth.

"Weiss!"

Dane's eyes flew open at Charlie Bingham's irate bellow. Keeley's lips spread in a sly smile and resumed speed. Dane bit back a groan of renewed excitement.

Charlie banged on the bathroom door. "Are you in there, Weiss?"

Dane didn't dare breathe. Keeley had slipped a finger behind his balls and was pressing on an agonizingly erotic bundle of nerves. He tensed, teetering on the edge of orgasm. He looked at his cock and she had marked him with her red lipstick and it was the sexiest thing he'd ever seen. Oh, no, oh, no, if he came and Charlie heard him, he'd know, he'd know exactly what Dane was doing, he was coming, coming, coming hard…he shuddered and gasped silently, spilling helplessly into Keeley's welcoming mouth. She swallowed him easily, his juices making his dick slide even more. *Oh, yes, sexy Keeley, take me, never let me go, oh, baby, suck me dry….*

Charlie called to someone passing the office. "If you see Mr. Weiss, tell him I want to see him right away. Arrogant SOB," he muttered. His steps faded as he left.

Dane could only pant and cling to the sink for several seconds after Charlie left. Keeley licked the corners of her mouth. "You're delicious, Dane. I could eat you up."

His knees weakened all over again. He'd been called lots of things, but "delicious" was a first. And eating him up? Hot damn.

"Dane? Are you all right?" Keeley stood and looked at him in concern. "You aren't saying anything. And we both know that's unusual."

"I'm fine," he managed to gasp. It was a lie. He was anything but fine. She looked great, except for some smeared lipstick.

She went on tiptoe to hug him and started to kiss him before pulling back. "Whoops, I might get some lipstick on your collar." She laughed merrily. "Although I think most of it wiped off somewhere else." She washed and dried her hands briskly. "I'll go fix my lipstick and get you a cup of coffee from the break room. That should give you enough time to get to your desk. Okay?"

He nodded dumbly. After she slipped out the bathroom door, he turned to face the mirror and reeled in shock. His face was sweaty and almost purple from biting back his cries, his hair sticking up in damp clumps. His makeup-smeared dick still jutted through the fly of his damp boxer shorts and was sensitive to the point of pain, as he realized trying to clean off Superstay lipstick with paper towels that he planned to hide in the absolute bottom of the wastebasket. He could have used his private shower but had no change of clothes and was afraid the staff might wonder why their new controller needed a shower at 10:00 a.m. on a Monday morning.

Dane zipped as best as he could and stared at his grim expression. So much for his hotshot talk about not mixing business with pleasure, leaving sex out of the office and in the bedroom.

Having a mind-blowing orgasm into his sexy pseudosecretary's mouth with his immediate supervisor in the next room was definitely a career first for Dane. And the frightening thing was, he couldn't wait for her do it again, except of course for the Charlie part.

When Dane went off the rails, he did it in a big way. Keeley had certainly shown him who was boss, and it wasn't Dane Weiss.

KEELEY COULDN'T keep a big grin off her face as she strolled through the rows of cubicles toward the office kitchen where the coffee was usually fresh. She carried Dane's giant University of Wisconsin mug to the sink and rinsed out the dregs of his first cup of the day.

"You're the new controller's assistant, right?"

Keeley turned to see a petite woman dressed in Bingham-approved attire, a charcoal-gray business pantsuit with a white blouse under it. Her blond hair was clipped into a ponytail at the nape of her neck. "That's right, I'm Cherry."

"I figured. Not many women would dare wear a fun outfit like yours to a morgue like this. By the way, I'm Teddy."

Keeley cocked her head in surprise to hear such heresy. "Glad you like it. I've got more where this one came from."

"Cool." Teddy turned her back to Keeley and lifted her ponytail. She'd had her hair buzzed short a couple inches above her nape and a hollow-eyed skull tattoo sat right below her hairline. "See, you're not the only rebel around here. I just crush my sense of personal individuality to make a boatload of cash to pay off my student loan vultures." Teddy leaned in close. "If you think that tat's cool, you should see the one right above my ass."

"No, thanks." Keeley couldn't help but laugh. "But hey, a girl's gotta do what a girl's gotta do."

"Ain't that a fact. Working at the Financial Firm of the Living Dead isn't a dream come true, but I'm learning a lot from these geezers. Someday, I'll start my own firm."

"Look me up when you're ready. I have a friend you can talk with." Teddy and Sugar would be a perfect fit. "Then you can make a ton of money and throw it around like the men here must do," Keeley fished around.

Teddy shrugged. "You'd think so, but most of these guys have expensive cars, expensive homes, expensive wives and expensive girlfriends—sometimes all four at once."

"Hmm." Talkative Teddy could be a gold mine of information. "I suppose people can dig themselves out of their money problems. Anyone who was broke before now and isn't now?"

"Yeah, funny you should mention that. Bob in accounting was always complaining about his kids' college tuition bills, but he just got back from a fancy European Riviera cruise. Said he inherited some money from an aunt."

"Boy, I wish I had a rich aunt." Bob from accounting was about to have his financial records turned upside down.

Teddy sighed. "You and me both. But hey, someday we'll have loads of money and we can look back and wonder how we ever worked here." She caught sight of the clock. "Oh, well. Back to the salt mines. I'm at extension 754 if you ever want to go out after work. I know this great bar with superhot guys who *don't* work here. FYI, I wouldn't touch most of the younger guys here with a ten-foot cattle prod. Bunch of pigs."

"I know the type." Keeley already had her own superhot guy, but Teddy would be fun to hang out with. Aside from Sugar and a couple of girls from the Love Shack, Keeley hadn't hung out with anyone since her CPA graduation. "Call me at Dane Weiss's office. I'd like to get together."

"That's right, you work for him." Teddy winked at her as she poured herself a cup of coffee. "I can understand if you're too busy to go out."

Keeley laughed. "I'll make time. Just let me know."

"Will do." Teddy lifted her mug in a toast and left the kitchen.

Keeley turned back to the coffee machine and filled Dane's giant mug with the last of the coffee. She wanted to give him some time to recover, so she busied herself making a new pot.

The look on his face when she'd finished pleasuring him with her mouth could only be described as stunned, but Keeley was stunned herself. She'd never done anything so wild, so wanton.

Lost in thought about Dane as well as her next step in investigating nouveau-riche Bob, Keeley carried the coffee mug plus some sugar and stirrers out of the kitchen. She knew now that Dane liked his coffee sweet.

She approached Glenn the controller's office and was surprised to hear his voice pleading with someone over the phone. He must have been using his secretary's phone in the outer office. "No, don't do that. I'll have your money, I promise."

Keeley strategically dropped her sugar packets and coffee stirrers onto the floor just out of visual range, but well within hearing.

She knelt and slowly gathered coffee stirrers as Glenn continued, "I understand I've put you in a bad position, and believe me, I'll make it up to you. Please, just a few more days. My wife will divorce me if this doesn't go through."

The other person must have agreed to an extension because Glenn thanked him fervently before hanging up. Keeley finished picking up her supplies and found a trashcan for the stirrers. She caught Glenn's eyes as she passed and nodded politely. He nodded back, his face still tense and drawn.

Keeley hurried back to her office, excited to tell Dane of the new avenues for their investigation but didn't see him at his desk. "Dane?" She poked her head into his bathroom, but he was gone.

Well, that was okay. She would get started on the high-end accounts Glenn and Bob had access to. Feeling energized, Keeley logged into her software and went to work. When Dane got back, she could show him they were finally making progress.

Dane didn't reappear until close to one o'clock.

"Hello, Mr. Weiss."

His expression was as stormy as the evening they'd gotten stuck in the elevator. "Come into the office, please, Cherry."

She stood and followed him. He closed the door behind her. "What's going on, Dane?" Had Charlie overheard Dane in the bathroom? Keeley hadn't meant to cause such a potentially compromising situation, but she had also wanted to regain some of the control she'd given up by making love with Dane.

He gave her a sour look. "Charlie, either in his infinite wisdom or else more likely petty revenge, has informed me I am going to London on the red-eye tonight. I won't be home until Saturday."

"Oh." No fun with Dane for the next five days.

"'Oh' is right. I don't want to go, but I can't refuse."

She nodded. "It would look strange. After all, he is your boss for the time being."

"And how is your project coming? Do you have anything yet?"

"Binky got me copies of Charlie's financial records, but they're complicated thanks to all his investments and inheritances. I did find several large cash withdrawals starting right after the new year. Charlie's a creature of habit, so they stick out." She also filled him in on Glenn's and Bob's money situations.

"Call the P.I. and get him to pull their bank records." He leaned close to her. "Come with me tonight. Have you ever seen London?"

London? Her only trip outside Illinois had been across the river to St. Louis. "I'd love to, but…"

His blue eyes lost their sparkle. "

"It's not that I don't want to go. I can't. I don't have a passport," she admitted almost shamefully.

"Really?"

She shook her head. He'd probably worn out several passports from all his traveling.

He rested his hand on her shoulder. "Would you have come with me otherwise, sweet Keeley?"

"Absolutely." Of course, considering how crazy they

were for each other, they probably wouldn't have seen much of London, but…

He groaned and squeezed her arm. "I'm going to miss you."

"Me, too." She looked at his handsome face and a lump of disappointment hardened in her chest.

He smiled at her. "Don't look at me like that, or I may tell Charlie to take his London trip and stick it."

"Look at you like what?" She'd tried her best to hide her growing feelings for him.

He rubbed his thumb daringly across her cheekbones. "With your sad green eyes."

She gave what sounded even to her an unconvincing laugh. "Come on, Dane, it's only for a few days. I have plenty to keep me busy while you're gone—Charlie's accounts and now Bob's and Glenn's."

"Good." Now it was his turn to look uncomfortable. "I know we didn't have a chance to discuss this yet, and I certainly don't want to make things awkward, but—" he took a big breath "—you should know I am not planning to look up any old girlfriends or see anyone while we're in this kind of a relationship."

"What kind of a relationship do you mean?"

He caught her teasing tone and relaxed. "A hot, sexy relationship where we can't keep our hands off each other and can't stop thinking about each other."

"I agree." As if any other man she met would measure up to Dane.

They spotted Mrs. Hobson passing the office and Dane pulled his hand off her. "Fine. Perhaps you could do a favor for me while I'm away on business, Miss Smith."

"Water your plants? Bring in your mail?"

"Not quite." He handed her a key chain, lowering his voice. "As soon as my plane touches down at O'Hare Saturday, I'm going to call you. I want you to go to my place and wait for me naked in my bed. Will you do that for me?"

Entranced, she could just nod wordlessly.

"Sweetheart, knowing I'll be with you as soon as I get home will be the only thing that gets me through this trip."

Inadvertently, she glanced at the bathroom door, and he followed her stare. "I wish I could, baby, but I have to go home and pack for my flight."

"I understand." She did understand, mentally sending Charlie Bingham to the devil. "Stay safe, Dane. I'll see you Saturday."

"Leave your phone on because you'll be hearing from me." He stared at her mouth. "Consider yourself kissed goodbye. I'll make it up to you Saturday."

"Bye, Dane." She made her way to her own desk, cheerfully waving him off when he left a couple minutes later.

The rest of the workweek stretched ahead of her in a mind-numbing, sexually barren bore. After several minutes staring blankly at her monitor, Keeley reflected on the downside of being good with numbers. That meant she could figure pretty much to the hour how long Dane would be away from her.

That was a disturbing idea. Less than three days after first sleeping with the man and she was counting the minutes until his return. Of course after they finished Binky's audit, Dane would be off on another job and Keeley would easily be able to calculate when he would come back. Never.

9

"I HAVEN'T BEEN OVER since you painted your place, Keeley." Sugar Jones looked around the living room as she lounged on Keeley's red-cushioned futon Tuesday night. "Who would think that purple walls would go so nicely with the red?"

Keeley looked up from the breakfast bar where she was arranging some ham mini-quiches and puff pastries stuffed with feta and spinach. "I painted it last Thanksgiving weekend. You really haven't been over since then?"

"Nope." Her friend shook her head, accepting a strawberry margarita fresh from the blender. "We've mostly seen each other at my loft or your office."

Keeley went to the kitchen and carried the appetizer tray to her glass-topped chrome coffee table. "I'm sorry about that. I never realized I was becoming such a hermit."

Sugar waved her apology away and snagged a quiche. "Don't worry about it, Keel. I know you were superbusy with your business, and I had a pretty heavy course load this past semester anyway. Only one more semester to go for my MBA."

"Good for you." Keeley, better than anybody, knew how hard it was to work her way through school, especially dancing crazy hours late into the night.

"I'm going to start a consulting business focusing on the entertainment industry here in Chicago. Nightclubs, bars, even the strip clubs. Are you interested in more accounting clients? You're about the only one I know who can make heads or tails out of some of those books."

"Which set of books? The ones for the IRS or the real ones?" Keeley asked dryly, picking up a spinach puff.

Sugar laughed. "I take it you'll pass. That's okay. Once Binky starts recommending you to more of his buddies, you'll have more business than you can handle. How's it going, by the way?"

"It's going okay. I'm making some progress but this really needs a team of auditors since there are at least three subjects to investigate. He's paying me a bundle to look through all these invoices, bank statements and requisition requests, but I haven't found anything conclusive yet."

"Don't worry about the money, honey. Binky told me he doesn't care how much it costs to find the truth."

Easy for Binky to say—he had plenty of dough. "The truth is, it could be almost anyone—Charlie, several upper-management guys, probably even some people I have no idea about." Keeley bit into her puff and brushed pastry crumbs off her green Chicago University sweatshirt. As soon as she came home from work, she had taken off her uncomfortable clothes and immediately changed into sweats and fuzzy socks.

"*Cherchez la femme,* that's what I always say," Sugar stated.

"What?" Keeley had studied Spanish in school, not French.

"It means 'Look for the woman.' You and I both

know we ladies are severely underestimated by the masculine sex."

"Ya think? But I haven't even found if thefts are occurring. It's worse than looking for a needle in a haystack—there may be a needle, or there may not be, or the needle is in the haystack near the cow barn instead of in the field."

Sugar eyed her with amusement. "My goodness, I can't even imagine where all these farm metaphors are popping up from."

The oven timer beeped and Keeley gladly hopped up to get the minipizzas. Her friend would return to *that* subject, she was sure.

"Is that a new poster, Keel?" Sugar stood and wandered over to the wall.

"Yep," Keeley called from the kitchen. "It's Mikhail Baryshnikov, the Russian ballet dancer, probably the best male dancer in the world. He's dancing *The Nutcracker* there." She shoved the pizzas off the pizza stone onto a platter to join the other snacks.

Sugar gave her a wicked glance over her margarita glass. "Is that the name of the ballet or his tights?"

"Sugar!" Keeley couldn't help giggling.

"I'm serious," she protested. "You think our dancing outfits are something? That guy's package is wrapped tighter than a gift under the Christmas tree."

"I'd give anything to dance with him."

"Why *don't* you dance anymore, Keeley? I don't mean at the club, I mean real dancing. Lessons, tights, recitals, the whole thing."

"Are you kidding, Sugar? Have you ever seen a six-foot-tall ballerina? I'm taller than all these guys and weigh more than them to boot." She'd loved her ballet lessons until she'd grown too tall and too busty for her instructor's liking. Then Madame Ludmilla had suggested she join the high school pom-pom squad, crushing her classical dance hopes. Old bag.

"You ever hear of modern dance, Miss Smarty-Pants? The guys don't have to heft you around. Hell, in some of those troupes you could probably lift the men and call it cutting-edge choreography." Sugar blew on a minipizza to cool it.

"Maybe some other time, Sugar. I've got a lot on my plate." Keeley demonstrated that by loading her plate with treats. Her spandex skirts could take it.

"You must be very busy, Keeley," Sugar said slyly. "I tried to call you over the weekend to see if you wanted to go out, but all I got was your voice mail. Were you working on Binky's project?"

"Yep."

"With Dane Weiss."

"Yep."

"Working *long* and *hard?* Pounding away at the sheets? Oops, I mean spreadsheets." Sugar tucked her foot under her and sat on the futon.

"Sugar..." Keeley's face heated.

Her friend whooped in laughter. "So you *did* take my advice regarding the big, brawny Mr. Weiss. Tell me, Keeley, is he brawny everywhere?"

"Oh, my God!" Keeley squealed, pressing her glass to her cheeks.

"Well?"

"Yes," she muttered. She tried to frown at Sugar's peals of laughter but a big, cheesy grin spread over her face. "But don't you dare say anything to anyone. Especially his sister."

"Honey!" Sugar gave her a shocked look. "When it comes to men, I am the soul of discretion. And besides, Bridget really does not want to know a thing about her brother's sex life. According to her, he's a strictly temporary man, flying in for a brief layover and flying out, so to speak."

"Oh." Keeley fought back unreasonable disappointment. She had known that from the first, after all.

"On the other hand, you have him stuck here in Chicago for as long as the audit takes, so take advantage of him. Which begs the question—why am I here tonight and not the magnificent Dane?"

Keeley stretched her legs and crossed her ankles. "He went to London Monday afternoon and won't be home until Saturday."

"Oh, I see. The puzzle pieces fall into place." Sugar nodded knowingly.

"What pieces?"

"Tonight, I am the platonic equivalent of a booty call," she announced grandly.

"A booty call?" Keeley sputtered into her cranberry martini.

"Boyfriend out of town? Call Sugar for company. I have been reduced to the infamous backup plan." She shook her head in mock sadness, her eyes twinkling.

"I prefer to think of it as a girls' night in." Keeley poured her another drink. "Eat, drink and be merry *without* men."

"Oh, yeah, you're real merry without Dane," Sugar scoffed. "Why on earth is the man in London anyway?

He should have offered to take you. Binky wouldn't have minded you guys taking a couple days off during the audit. The old guy's a romantic at heart."

"Charlie sent Dane to England, and I couldn't go because I don't have a passport."

Sugar pursed her lips. "That Charlie loves to wreck everybody's fun. He has a cow every time Binky takes me out on the town. Probably needs to get laid."

"You offering? He's not bad-looking." Keeley figured it was time for Sugar to get a little teasing back.

"No way! He's so uptight he probably squeaks when he thrusts. Although I do like unbuttoning a buttoned-up man…." Sugar lapsed into a brief reverie while Keeley watched her speculatively. Her friend shook her head and snapped out of it. "But we were talking about *you*."

"Why do you think I changed the subject?" Keeley retorted. "Enough about that. I'm thinking of painting the kitchen a really retro aqua."

"What does Dane think about that?" Sugar ate another miniquiche. "And what does he think of Mr. Nutcracker over there?"

Keeley shrugged. "He doesn't think anything about either of them. He's never been here."

Sugar's eyes widened. "Not even when he picks you up or drops you off?"

"Nope. Parking's been a real problem lately, so I hop in or out. No big deal. We were just, you know, *together* for a few days before he left."

"You haven't invited him in because of lack of parking?" Sugar crinkled her nose. "Look, I can understand being cautious with a guy when you're first *together,* as it were, but Dane's a real straight arrow. I remember him from when he used to drive Binky to the clubs, and he was always respectful to the girls, actually kept his hands to himself."

"Fine." According to Sugar's previous debriefing, he had worked for Binky as a driver/bodyguard/babysitter while he went to school, but she still didn't want to think about Dane in the strip clubs.

"Have you told him, you know?" Sugar made a broad gesture. "How you got through school?"

Keeley set down her puff, suddenly not hungry. "No. He knows I worked in a bar-type place but I made it seem like I was a bookkeeper or waitress or something like that."

"Not quite the whole truth."

"I don't *need* to tell him the truth, the whole truth and nothing but the truth, Sugar. I'm not under oath with him." Just because Sugar enjoyed a life in the spotlight, didn't mean Keeley did. "Give me a break. I slept with the guy for the first time last Friday. I'll tell him I used to be a stripper when you tell me your real first name." Sugar was like Rumplestiltskin in that regard, horrified to tell anyone her real name.

"Okay, okay, no reason to get snippy. I just don't want you to get sandbagged if someone from Bingham Brothers recognizes you with your old wig. Some of those guys are real aficionados and might remember you and your whipped-cream act."

"Ugh. I probably helped destroy a good part of the ozone layer with all those aerosol cans." Her joke helped lighten the mood and they both laughed.

Sugar helped herself to another margarita from the purple glass pitcher. "And for heaven's sake, apply for a rush-job passport. If Dane asks you on another trip, *go*. A man like him is easy pickings, you know. You got him all sexed up and now he's cut off."

"Him? What about me?" Keeley cried indignantly. "I didn't have sex for a whole eighteen months previously and now *I'm* cut off!" It was true. She'd been twitchy, irritable and lying awake at night for lack of him.

"Sorry, sweetie. Despite what I may do onstage, the whole girl thing doesn't do it for me at all. You're on your own, if you know what I mean."

"I do," Keeley replied sourly. "And for the record, I wasn't propositioning you." Unlike Sugar, she'd never even done "girl" stuff onstage.

"Good!" Sugar tipped back her drink and smacked her lips. "Things get so complicated when sex comes into the picture, don't they?"

Keeley stuffed a puff into her mouth and nodded in agreement. "Ain't that the truth."

KEELEY WANDERED THROUGH the office Wednesday morning during the ten o'clock break as she sipped her mug of coffee. Her meandering was actually purposeful as she was aiming toward the accounting department.

Teddy's tip had been a good starting point, but there were at least three Bobs in accounting. The P.I. obviously needed a last name, not wanting to track down all the Bobs in Chicago who had an aunt die somewhere in the world sometime in the past year or so. Even Binky didn't have enough money to pay for an investigator like that.

Keeley had never been to accounting before, but it matched what she'd seen in other big companies—rows of cubicles in the center with management's offices on the perimeter. She strolled up and down the aisles, trying to spot nameplates. John, Mark, Bill, Curt, Debbie—wow, an actual female name, Jeff, Dirk—bet he thought he was all that and a bag of chips, Bob—bingo.

Bob wasn't in his cubicle. Keeley tried to see if there were any recent vacation photos featuring him on a cruise.

"Hey, there," a male voice said behind her.

Keeley turned. "Hey." It was one of the more tenacious losers who had crowded around her desk for several days after her arrival at Bingham Brothers.

"Cherry, right?" The dark-haired guy leaned casually on the cubicle wall.

"Right, umm…" She couldn't remember his name.

"Dirk." He pointed at the cubicle next to Bob's. "Nice to see you again. What brings you to our neck of the woods?"

"I'm here to see Bob."

His expression was priceless. "Bob? This Bob?" He pointed into the cubicle.

"Maybe. If he's the Bob who just got back from a European cruise."

"Oh. That's Bob Petrocelli. He sits over in the far corner." He gestured toward the back of the department.

She nodded sympathetically. "I heard his aunt just died."

Dirk shrugged. "Something like that. I guess she wanted him to see the old country and left him money for a cruise to Italy."

Sounded plausible, and thank goodness his last name wasn't Smith or Jones. Petrocelli would be much easier to track.

"So how do you take your coffee?" Dirk the Drip used his inane question as an excuse to give her the once-over with his eyes.

Keeley didn't know whether to laugh or chuck the contents over him. "I take my coffee strong, thanks."

Dirk got the hint. "Right. Gotta get back to work." He went into his cubicle and stared intently at the screen.

She strolled off toward Bob's cubicle. This Bob was missing as well, but his desk held pay dirt. A photo of a middle-aged guy and family in front of the Roman Colosseum plus a funeral Mass card tacked up in loving memory of Francesca Maria Petrocelli De Luca.

"Can I help you?"

Keeley spun around. "Bob Petrocelli?"

"Yes?" He was a more serious version of his vacation picture, slightly balding with a spare tire, but with warm brown eyes.

"I'm Cherry Smith, Mr. Weiss's assistant." She examined him for flinching or other signs of guilt.

His expression was calm. "Oh, yes, I met him his first week. Does he need anything?"

"No, I heard you just got back from Italy and was wondering if you would recommend the company you went with."

His face lit up. "Absolutely. We had a wonderful time. Thanks to my dear aunt's legacy, we had the chance." He chattered about Rome and Florence, even going as far as to write down the cruise line's name and his travel agent's phone number.

"Well, thanks a lot, Bob. I appreciate it."

He waved off her thanks. "Everyone should see Italy before they die. You'll never be the same."

Keeley smiled. Maybe she could take Lacey for a college graduation present in a few years. She left accounting, reviewing the new information she could pass on to the P.I. He'd be sure to check it out thoroughly, but if Bob Petrocelli was lying, Keeley was a natural redhead.

"WELCOME TO Chicago's O'Hare International Airport. Please check for all your possessions. The local time is nineteen hundred hours or 7:00 p.m. Thank you for flying with us, and we look forward to serving you again." The cabin attendant clicked off the seat belt sign and Dane grabbed for his cell phone, his big fingertips fumbling over the keys in his eagerness to call Keeley.

They had e-mailed business files back and forth the past several days, but had both stayed away from any personal conversation by tacit agreement. He wasn't quite sure why. Maybe her feelings had cooled and she didn't know how to gracefully dump him. He hoped not. In his case, his desire for her had grown, but he didn't want to seem pathetic, panting long-distance after a woman he'd only been involved with for a few days.

Keeley answered on the first ring, just as Dane had hoped. "Hello?"

"It's me, baby." He had to raise his voice to be heard over the other transatlantic passengers gathering their gear.

"Dane." Her voice softened and trembled a tiny bit. "Where are you?"

"O'Hare airport, concourse M. Will you meet me at my place?"

"Dane, I'm already here. Come home to me as soon as you can." She hung up.

Home to Keeley. Where he always wanted to go. The

thought stopped him as suddenly as if it were a suitcase falling onto his head. He had been dreaming about coming home to her the whole past week in England. Being without her had made London seem like the most boring burg in rural America.

One British passenger coughed politely behind him, and Dane snapped out of his stupor. The sooner he deplaned, the sooner he'd be with Keeley and get all this sappy, longing-type stuff out of his system.

Caught up in his thoughts, he stumbled over the uneven walkway.

"Careful, sir." The steward caught his elbow. "You don't want to fall."

"No, I don't," Dane agreed. Fall on the concourse *or* fall for Keeley.

KEELEY HUNG UP her cell phone and fought the urge to jump in glee. Dane had arrived and called her just as he said he would. She had let herself in to his fancy condo an hour earlier after checking his flight status online.

She had been too antsy to do any more work, so she'd taken a long, hot bath in the whirlpool tub, anticipating his return. As the spicy-scented bubbles caressed her body, she'd been tempted to take the edge off her desire, but decided to wait for Dane. She brushed her hair and applied some glittery scented lotion, lighting several matching scented candles in Dane's bedroom.

She turned off the crystal chandelier and the flickering candlelight made the room cozy and warm instead of brilliant and sharp. Once her lotion had soaked in, she shucked off her robe and climbed naked into Dane's bed.

The sheets were chilly on her skin and she shivered, partly from nerves. She'd never waited naked for a man in his bed before. Mostly because she had never wanted to for anyone else. But she found herself doing things because of Dane that she hadn't anticipated. Maybe Sugar was right, and Keeley should explain her background to him. That way, if he got upset about it, she'd only have spent a week or so as his lover. No harm, no foul.

Yeah, right. Like *that* would help.

The front door opened with a thud. "Keeley?" his baritone voice called. "Where are you?"

"Right here, Dane." She clutched his heavy golden silk bedding to her bare breasts as his footsteps thudded through the condo.

He stopped in the doorway in his tan cashmere coat, his blond hair adorably mussed by the spring winds, a grin spreading over his face. "You *are* here." He shrugged his expensive coat to the floor and began undressing. "What are you wearing?"

"Some glittery lotion and a smile." She grinned at him.

"My favorites." He unbuttoned his rumpled blue shirt and kicked his shoes off. "Did you miss me, Keeley?"

"Were you gone?" she asked with mock surprise.

"Was I gone?" He stopped unbuckling his belt and shook his head in disbelief. "You're gonna get it now. I bet you counted the minutes until I got back, didn't you?"

"No." She shook her head. She hadn't counted the minutes—more like the hours.

He shoved down his pants and boxers and stalked toward the bed, powerfully erect. She was quivering in anticipation as he yanked the covers off and practically drooled over her naked body. "Oh, Keeley, how did I ever leave you?" He turned north and shook his fist in the air. "Curse you, Charlie Bingham, you cruel bastard, you!"

Keeley burst out laughing while Dane pulled a condom from his nightstand. She already had three tucked under her pillow.

"I distinctly remember leaving you unfulfilled." He sheathed himself. "I've spent the whole week thinking how to make it up to you. Sitting in meetings with stuffy English businesspeople wondering what sexy outfit you were wearing to work and imagining how quickly I could take you out of it. Looks like you beat me to the punch." He bent and kissed her on the mouth.

Keeley sighed in pleasure and wrapped her arms around his neck. He quickly eased her to a semi-reclining position on the mountain of pillows and positioned himself between her thighs. "You are so beautiful. I oughta have my head examined for going away."

She hooked her legs around his calves. "Don't go away again. I mean, not for a while anyway," she hastily corrected.

"I promise." He guided himself to her folds and eased into her. "You're already wet. Were you thinking about me?" He pressed in farther.

"Maybe." She closed her eyes in bliss.

He stopped. "Maybe? Baby, give me a break. I've been frightening the good citizens of London with my inappropriate hard-ons for the past week and all you can give me is a 'maybe'?"

She opened her eyes and giggled. "You were *not* walking around London with a hard-on."

"Only due to my iron will. Now I'm not going to

move an inch until you tell me you were thinking about me all week, too."

That hit too close to the mark. She'd been a mope since he was gone. "Yes, I thought of you. Quite a lot."

"I guess I'll take 'quite a lot' as the right answer." He moved in her again.

She dug her fingers into his shoulders. "More than quite a lot," she whispered. "All the time."

"Really," he purred. "At night?" He brushed her clit with his big finger. "Did you do this to yourself, Keeley? Did you think of me and touch yourself?"

She buried her face into his chest and nodded. More than once, in fact.

"Did you imagine me hot and hard inside of you like this?" His erotic-book-narrator tone was back as he dug deep, pressing her into the pillows.

"Yes."

"Good. Because I imagined you hot and wet above me, your pretty pink lips gasping as I played with your tits." He bent and kissed her nipple, flicking the tip with his tongue. "You made me so crazy right before I left. I couldn't stop thinking of you." He sounded almost angry as he sped his thrusts.

"Me, either." Keeley ground her hips into him and bit his earlobe, making him gasp in pleasure. "All I did was calculate what time it was in London and wonder what you were doing."

"You better come with me next time." He rolled to his back, taking her with him. She immediately moved on him as he played with her breasts, just like he'd fantasized. His thumbs brushed over her nipples and she clenched his cock.

"I'll come with you all the time," she promised.

He stroked her ass and squeezed while his other hand found her clit. "Ride me, baby."

Keeley smiled and cupped her breasts, teasing and pulling at her nipples until they were as hard and throbbing as Dane's cock deep inside her. She reached behind her and squeezed his balls the way he liked it.

His fingers dug into her hips and his face tightened. "Oh, yeah, honey." He plucked at her clit until her pussy tightened around him.

"Oh, Dane…" She braced her free hand on his broad chest as she writhed on top of him, her orgasm pounding through her as the pent-up sexual frustration of the past week broke free. She almost cried from the relief of having him back with her, back inside her. Ducking her head, she hid her face from him, suddenly aware of her vulnerability to him. Not just physically, but emotionally, too.

She must have inadvertently tightened her grip on him because he came with a groan, his balls lifting and pulsing under her hand. "Sexy Keeley, don't stop. I need you so bad." The words were almost dragged from him unwillingly.

She rode him until he was gasping for mercy and collapsed onto him. The perfume of the candles and their lovemaking filled the air. He kissed the top of her head. "Maybe I should go away more often."

Keeley gave a little laugh, and rested her head on his chest. As she listened to the steady thump of his heart, an unfamiliar contentment came over her, settling her usually keyed up mind. She wrapped her arms around him and closed her eyes. Dane was home with her where he belonged.

10

DANE STARED INTO his freezer trying to decide what to eat for dinner. It was his first evening on his own since he got home from London a couple of days ago. Keeley was speaking about security of financial accounts at a women-in-business networking dinner, so he was obviously not invited.

Keeley had everything under control at work, eliminating one of their suspects—some poor schmuck in accounting who'd actually been on the up-and-up. Glenn, the man who was mentoring Dane, was still on their list of possibilities, and that made Dane uneasy. Dane was a straightforward kind of guy, and he found it difficult to not just come out and ask Glenn about any money troubles.

Dane dug out a frozen pasta entrée and popped it in the microwave, drumming his fingers on the granite countertop as it heated. He tasted it when it was done and grimaced. The gooey sauce had spilled onto everything and, like most people, Dane didn't care for tomato-flavored spiced apples. So not only did he have to eat a crappy dinner, he had to eat it alone.

He muttered a curse and chucked the unappetizing meal in the trash. He was looking for the pizza delivery menu when his cell phone rang. Maybe Keeley had gotten out of her meeting early. He checked the caller ID. No such luck. "Hey," he answered.

"Lovely to talk to you, too, Dane," his sister Bridget retorted.

"Sorry, Bridge. I was in the middle of something."

"That's okay. Remember my telling you I was going to Wisconsin to work on my wedding plans with Mom?"

"Uh-huh." He'd forgotten, actually.

"So she sent me back with some stuff for you. Can I drop if off now?"

He sighed. "Sure, why not. I'll tell the doorman to send you up."

She laughed. "When we were growing up on the farm, did you ever think you'd have a doorman?"

"Are you kidding? I thought a doorman was the guy who held the door for the cows as they moved in and out of the milking parlor." He checked his watch. "When will you be here?"

"Give me half an hour."

"See you then." Dane hung up and called the pizza place and the doorman to let him know about both his pizza and his sister.

As he walked into the living room to flip channels, he wondered what Keeley was doing. He checked his watch. Probably eating dinner or drinking one of those fruity martinis she favored. Tipping back her head as she drank, her pretty brown waves of hair brushing her shoulders… Dane shook his own head in disgust. Mooning over his girlfriend when he'd just seen her a couple hours ago.

Girlfriend? He almost walked into a marble column in his living room. Why had that word popped into his head? What *was* Keeley to him?

His analytical mind finally kicked into gear. Keeley was A, his coworker, B, his partner in fighting financial crime, C, the woman he made love to on a regular basis, D, the woman he couldn't stop thinking about, E, the woman he dreamed about…wow. That was a girlfriend, all right.

Well. Dane dropped heavily onto the big leather couch. He had a girlfriend. It had been years since he'd considered any woman that. Not since college at least. A big cheesy grin cracked his face and he knew he must look like a real sap.

He was still smiling when the pizza arrived and then his sister a few minutes later. She greeted him with a hug and pulled back quizzically, her wavy blond hair pulled into a clip, her cheeks pink from the perpetual lake breeze. They resembled each other more than their brother Colin, who was dark-haired. "You certainly look more cheerful than you sounded before."

"Do I?" He frowned theatrically. "This better?"

"Oh, you." She handed him a medium-size cardboard box and slugged him in the arm. "From Mom. Not that you deserve it or anything."

"Thanks. Want some pizza?" He walked into the kitchen and set the box on the island.

"Sounds good." She followed, tossing her leather jacket on the couch, where it promptly slid to the floor. "Rats. You'd think I'd be used to these couches by now. I'm always sliding off Adam's."

"Ugh, I don't need to know that." Dane dished up several slices of pizza and poured his sister a glass of the diet root beer she preferred. He got himself a real beer and popped the cap.

She dusted off her jacket and set it on an upholstered chair. "Jealous you don't have anybody to slide off your own couch?"

His beer went down the wrong way and he choked for a few seconds while his sister pounded on his back a little too enthusiastically. "Okay, okay, I'm good." He raised his hands in self-defense.

"Dane Herbert Weiss." With that calculating expression on her face, Bridget looked uncannily like their mother. "You *do* have a couch-slider. Quick work. You've only been in Chicago for a few weeks."

"A couch-slider, Bridge?" He aimed for a casual laugh. "That's a new one on me."

"Never mind. I want to know as little as possible about your sex life."

"Ditto, in a big way." Dane sat at the modern glass kitchen table. "Bad enough I get Adam mooning over your upcoming wedding plans. Who do I look like, Miss Manners?"

"Not even close." Bridge eyed his gray sweatpants and red University of Wisconsin sweatshirt and sighed, but joined him at the table anyway. "At least you clean up nice. You'll look good in that wedding tux, if they can find one in your size."

"Thanks." He passed a plate of pizza to her and she dug in.

They ate in easy silence until Bridget let out a loud burp. Dane laughed. "Good one, Miss Manners."

"Stupid root beer." But she was smiling. "That's one advantage of designing my own wedding dress. I can allow for a couple slices of pizza here and there."

"I look forward to seeing your dress." Adam had

wondered ad nauseam about her wedding dress. Dane mostly nodded and thought about Keeley during his friend's monologues.

Bridget snickered. "You big liar. The only thing you'll notice about it is that it's long and white."

"Busted." He tipped back in his chair and grinned at her.

She looked around his kitchen. "You know, this is nice, Dane. Having dinner together like we did when we were kids. No fancy occasion, just pizza and root beer."

"Yeah, it is nice." Dane thought back, and he could count on one hand the number of times he and Bridget had even seen each other over the past couple of years. Bridget would like hanging out with Keeley, too. He vaulted his chair upright, uneasy at the thought of them meeting. "Dessert?"

"Sure."

He could feel her gaze on him as he rummaged in the freezer for gourmet chocolate ice cream bars. Keeley's favorite. He shut the door with a touch too much firmness and handed a bar to his sister.

"You okay, Dane?" She bit into the ice cream and swallowed. "Yum-oh. You seem out of sorts, edgy. Something on your mind?"

Not something, someone. "I've got a lot on my plate with my new job. It's a big change for me."

Bridget licked her dessert and nodded. "Controller-in-training for an institution like Bingham Brothers, and at your age? You're playing in the big leagues now." She laughed. "Mom's ecstatic you're actually living in one place for longer than a week. She wants you to settle down and produce several blond grand-kids for her."

He winced. "Great. I thought that was Colin's job. And yours. You're the one getting married, not me."

"I'm just the messenger, buddy." She tossed the bare stick on her plate. "But FYI, bring your own date to my wedding unless you want an endless stream of local maidens throwing themselves at you."

"Swell."

"I can't believe you don't have anyone in mind. Not even the girl who's sliding off your couch?"

"Drop it, Bridge."

"I see." She eyed him speculatively. "My wedding's only a couple months away, and you don't have to leave Chicago thanks to your new job. Get cracking and surely somebody will take pity on you."

He decided to get some of his own back for that pity crack. "I bet Sugar would be glad to set me up with one of her friends from work. They're all eager to meet young, successful professional men."

She pursed her lips and lowered her eyebrows. "Dane, if you come to my wedding with a stripper…"

"What? They're good enough for you as clients, but not socially?"

Bridge looked off to the side. "No, I mean, they are my friends, and Sugar is coming to the wedding. I guess you can go with her if you need to."

"Oh, can I? Thanks, sis." He cleared their places and put the leftovers in the fridge.

She stood and gave him a hug. He returned her embrace awkwardly. He'd never been much of a huggy guy. His baby sister reached on tiptoes to kiss his cheek. "Sorry for turning into Bridezilla for a minute. Dane, you bring whoever makes you happy."

"Thanks." He smiled down at her. "As soon as I find her, you'll know." *Liar,* a nagging voice called. *You already have found her.*

Bridget patted his shoulder and went to the box she'd brought. "Before I forget, Mom sent a set of crochet-topped kitchen towels for your new place." She lifted a white lacy bundle. Dane knew they'd be wrecked within a week if he ever dared use them. "A jar of home-canned Rainier cherries and a homemade cherry pie." She set the jar and pie plate on the counter.

A big grin spread over his face. He knew a certain lady with a weakness for cherry pie.

"Mom says to eat the pie this weekend before it gets stale," Bridget warned him.

"Don't worry, I'll get good use out of it," he promised.

She gave him a curious look, but Dane just smiled.

THE NEXT DAY, Keeley looked up from her computer screen and rolled her shoulders. The women-in-business get-together had been fun, but she had found herself wondering what Dane would think about this comment or if he would laugh at that joke.

Probably "no" for the jokes, since most of them were about men, and men in finance in particular. Keeley could have shared some really racy stories but her accounting acquaintances didn't know about her previous career.

And neither did Dane. She had been sitting way too long and was starting to get restless if *that* thought drifted across her mind. Dane sat across the big glass dining table, his stare intent on his own paperwork. She pulled off her computer glasses and eyed him up and down.

Man, was he handsome in only his navy terry cloth

robe and cotton knit boxer briefs. She took the opportunity to drink him in. His sun-streaked blond hair and
blue eyes, as bright as the spring sky. His dimples were
hidden for the moment, but his lips were smooth and
sculpted as a statue.

But she knew better than anyone how much of a flesh-
and-blood man he was. Her gaze trailed from his wide
shoulders to his muscled chest. He stopped absentmindedly to scratch his heavy thigh, and her heart pounded.

Now, she enjoyed auditing as much as the next accountant, but even the best had to take a break. She
stretched her hands over her head to let her coral-pink
silk robe fall open a bit to show her lace-trimmed ivory
cotton camisole top.

His gaze was instantly on her, especially the skin of
her breasts and belly revealed by her stretch. "How was
your cherry pie, baby?" He gestured at the sticky plate
in front of her.

"Delicious. I've never had homemade cherry pie
before and it was wonderful." She'd practically licked
the plate clean.

"My mom does make good pie, right from the cherry
orchard at the farm. You want another piece?"

"Maybe later." She gave a theatrical yawn. "But I'm
more bored than hungry right now. All those numbers."
She gave a mock pout.

He grinned at her. "I can't imagine where I got the
idea you liked numbers."

"All work and no play, you know." She stood and
circled around to him.

"Makes Keeley kinda, you know…" He tugged her
to sit on his lap. "Turned on?" he whispered into her ear.

"If you want me to take care of your problem, all you have to do is ask."

And it was true. In the past two weeks since they'd started sleeping together, he'd been insatiable for her. He'd made *her* insatiable for *him.* And that hadn't ever happened before. Despite all her experience at erotic pretense, the real thing had only happened with Dane. She'd always danced with her emotions shut off for her own protection, but what if she danced for someone she cared about? She hopped off his lap and moved away from him. "Let's play a game, Dane."

"What kind of game?" His dimples deepened in anticipation.

Her heart sped up. "Let's pretend you're at one of those clubs and I'm a dancer." It was as close as she could come to admitting her past.

"What kind of club?" He lifted an eyebrow.

"One of those clubs where women dance for men and get them all aroused."

"You don't have to dance for me to do that, Keeley. I think of you and I get aroused," he admitted with a quick smile. "But if you wanted to put those sexy red shoes on and enjoy yourself by dancing, I wouldn't mind watching."

Arousal made her motions shaky as she found the red shoes tossed in a corner and strapped them on. "Got some music?"

He picked up a remote control and turned on his stereo. She giggled at the first tune. "Love in an Elevator?"

He grimaced in embarrassment. "I've had that tune in my head for the past week or so."

"I can't imagine why." She'd danced to it more times than she could count, but this was the first time that mattered. Her hips swayed, her robe slipping off one shoulder and then the other before falling off completely. She expertly kicked it away and stood in her undies and racy shoes.

Judging from the rapt expression on Dane's face, he found her camisole and boy-cut panties just as sexy as Cherry's over-the-top getups. Her nipples hardened under the thin cotton and she hugged her arms under her breasts, plumping them up.

Her breath came faster as she did several turns across the marble floor. Dane had shifted slightly, his erection obvious under his briefs. She slowly lifted the hem of her top, revealing the bottom curves of her breasts and her button-hard nipples before tossing that garment aside as well.

She was inventing new moves as she went along, her feelings for Dane bubbling to the surface and inspiring her. She licked her finger and circled her nipple, feeling it swell even more. She tossed her head back in real arousal, cupping and squeezing her breasts until they flushed with blood. He groaned in response.

She turned her back to Dane and bent over slightly, resting her hands on her thighs. The music changed to "Love Shack" and she was glad Dane couldn't see her grin. Almost like old times, but she'd never enjoyed a dance as much as this one.

She gyrated her bottom at Dane, knowing full well how that move would drive him nuts. He was always grabbing her ass at the office when no one was looking and had her ride him like a cowgirl so he could caress her there.

"Oh, baby, yeah," he called hoarsely. "Work it, honey."

He hadn't seen anything yet. She hooked her thumbs under the elastic and shimmied her damp panties down, teasing him with a glimpse of each cheek before stripping entirely. At the strip club, she'd always left her G-string on, but Dane was in for a world premiere. Dancing strong, they called it, when a dancer went totally bare. You had to be strong to forgo even the pretense of clothing.

Totally naked except for her shoes, she widened her stance and grabbed an ankle in each hand. She bent over all the way and enjoyed the stunned expression on Dane's upside-down-appearing face. He had quite the view, and she knew he could tell how aroused she was.

"Just when I thought I knew how beautiful you were, you still surprise me."

She felt her face heat, hoping he would think it was gravity pulling the blood there. She straightened slowly and took a second to catch her breath, discombobulated and dizzy.

"Come here, baby."

She sashayed over to him, her balance and confidence returning. "You like what you see?"

"Oh, very much. Wanna sit on my lap, honey?" Judging from his erection, Keeley knew what kind of sitting he had in mind. He stroked the curve of her ass, stopping to tickle the hollow of her knee.

"I'm sorry, you're not allowed to touch the dancers."

"What if it's one dancer who is making me really hot?"

"No, you cannot, sir." Keeley spun away. "If you can't follow the rules, I'll have to call security." She strutted over to a load-bearing marble pillar and slung a leg around it. It was too wide to do some of the more interesting pole tricks, but she rubbed her aching nipples over the cold, smooth stone and shuddered in real desire.

"Keeley."

She pretended to ignore him, caressing the pillar as if it were his hard body. After a few seconds, Dane cleared his throat. She looked over to find a sly smile on his face as he ran his hand down his chest, below his navel, stopping at his waistband. He wouldn't, would he?

He would. He pulled the front of his briefs down. His big hand cupped his big cock, and he sighed in relief as he stroked its length. A rush of answering moisture dampened Keeley's thighs. He never touched himself in front of her before, not really needing to. She found it incredibly erotic as he worked the pole of flesh as she worked her pole, his nipples tightening in the mat of golden hair. His gaze never left hers, even as his left hand cupped and squeezed his heavy balls. Keeley could practically feel their weight from where she squirmed. "Now, sir, you're *really* not allowed to do that here."

"Consider it a compliment to your dancing skills." His shaft grew darker and darker with blood, and he finally broke eye contact when he tossed back his head and groaned. He was going to call her bluff and make himself come.

She let go of the column and walked shakily over to him. "Are you feeling all right? You're all flushed." Especially his cock.

He slowed his pace but didn't stop. "I'm fine. There's no law about fantasizing about beautiful dancers, is there?"

She spun his swivel chair to the side and dropped to her knees. Placing her hands on his thighs, she gazed at him with her most seductive expression. "We're trained to aid our customers if they are in distress." She brushed her lips over the tip of his penis. "Are you in distress, sir?" she asked huskily.

"Oh, extreme distress. I think I may die if you don't help me." He threaded his fingers through her hair and guided her to his erection. "You're my only hope."

Keeley settled her mouth around his cock and Dane groaned. He tasted slightly of soap and fully of man, clean and salty. She lapped and sucked at its head, smiling as it swelled. She tongued the slit, loving the little moan he made as more fluid leaked. Relaxing her throat, she took in as much of the shaft as she could and cupped the rest in her hand.

She mimicked his previous masturbation, bobbing her head with her sucks and working his balls in the palm of her hand. Feeling them tighten under her fingers, she knew he couldn't take much more. He had already been close to the edge when she started.

He confirmed her suspicions when he groaned her name. "Stop, I'm gonna…" She shook her head and kept going. He grasped briefly at her shoulders but fell back in the chair when she scraped the sensitive underside of his cock with her teeth. "Oh, yeah, baby, *don't* stop."

His powerful thighs tensed and quivered under her as the pressure built. Keeley gave him one last powerful suck and he blasted into her mouth, crying her name, her real name, never Cherry's.

She kept at him through his long orgasm, only stopping when he caught her and eased her away. She wiped her mouth and stared greedily at his drained cock, its jerking and pulsing creating answering sensations in her pussy. Almost subconsciously, she crept her hand down her belly right above her strip of hair.

Dane opened his eyes and caught her wrist before she could relieve the ache. "My poor Keeley. Got yourself all worked up." He stood and swung her into his arms. "You're not going to take care of it that easily."

He strode through the apartment and set her at the side of his bed while he yanked off the coverings. "Lie down. If I catch you touching yourself, I'll tie you to the bedposts."

Not bothering to see if she obeyed, he left the room. Should she go along with the game? It had quickly spiraled past anything she'd imagined, but either way she played it, she'd be a winner.

She lay down in his big king-size bed, the sheets cool against her skin. She absentmindedly rubbed an itchy spot on her collarbone.

"Caught you." Dane stood with a dinner tray in the doorway.

"I was itchy!" she protested, not sure about being tied up.

"Okay," he said grudgingly. "Besides, if I tie you up, I might not be able to do some of the things I have planned."

"When did you plan any of this?" Keeley gestured at the tray, which looked like it held the leftover fruit pie and something covered with a napkin.

"The only time I'm not planning wild sexual games with you is when I'm actually doing wild sexual things with you." He set down the tray. "No, scratch that. I think of other ways to make love to you when I'm inside you, wondering how you'd like me to bend you over my desk, or wondering if you'd like my tongue in your pussy."

Keeley inhaled a shocked breath at his words. He smiled at her in satisfaction. "That last one? Yeah, I thought so." He swiped a fingerful of cherry pie filling and smeared it on her nipples, which beaded even further.

"Ooh, Dane, that's cold!" She started to rise to her elbows but he shook his head.

"You're so hot, you'll warm it in no time." He continued to paint her breasts and belly with the filling, drawing erotic swirls on her. He finally set a cherry in her belly button and tugged her so her bottom was on the foot of the bed. "Open your legs for me and close your eyes, baby."

She did as he wanted, hoping he would paint her there, too. Instead, something round and hard brushed her clit. Her eyes flew open. "Dane?"

He grinned at her and held up a small yellow fruit touched with red. "Rainier cherries. The cream of the crop, the sweetest of the sweet. But not as sweet as you." He licked the cherry, his blue eyes never leaving hers. "Your juices taste much better." A rush of warmth ran to her pussy, and her hips rocked. He smiled at her response. "I have something you'll like, my sweet Keeley."

She gasped as he pushed the cold fruit inside her. "What are you doing?"

"Filling you." He pushed one after another into her. She inadvertently clenched around his fingers, the cherries shifting and rubbing her inside as she moaned.

"That's it. Let the cherries tease you as I eat the rest of you." He bent over her breasts and licked the filling from one nipple, tugging the tip until it swelled in his mouth.

Keeley ran her fingers through his short blond hair, holding him close to her. Dragging his tongue across her, he ate her other breast clean. Every tug of his mouth and flick of his tongue spun ribbons of excitement through her cherry-filled pussy, the firm roundness of the cherries tormenting her. "Too much, Dane."

He shook his head, his breath hot and sweet on her exquisitely sensitized skin. "No backing out now. If you like these, I'll buy you a set of the metal balls." He knelt on the floor between her legs and ate the cherry from her belly button, his mouth dipping and sucking on the indentation.

"I'll put them inside you at the office and make you sit at your desk. Every time you shift, you'll want to come. But if you leave them there all morning, I'll take pity on you and fuck you at lunch." Dane brushed his finger over her clit. "Bent over the sink with your breasts bare." He stopped to pinch her nipples, still sticky from his mouth. "And your ass tipped up to my cock, as I pull out the metal balls and fill you with me."

He lifted one leg and kissed and nibbled all the way from her ankle strap to behind her knee and hooked it over his broad shoulder. He did the same to the other leg. Keeley saw him kneeling between her thighs, smiling at her, her sexy red shoes making the sensual scene even more erotic. It was as if she had been dancing for a private client and had become so aroused she let him make love to her.

Keeley groaned as he finally did what she was desperate for and put his mouth on her pussy.

He tongued her clit as if it were a cherry itself, stroking and playing with it. His hands stroked her thighs and bottom.

He dipped into her passage and sucked out a cherry,

chewing it with his strong white teeth. "Delicious." He repeated that several times, reaching in with his fingers and teasing her as he pulled out the fruits. Keeley writhed as the pressure in her vagina constantly shifted.

"One more, baby, tucked deep in your pussy." He teased it out. "Taste yourself." He held the cherry between his teeth and bent to her mouth.

She hesitated for a second, but he brushed it across her lips. She took a bite, her juices mixing salty with the sweet. He ate the rest of the cherry and kissed her hard, the scent of her on his lips incredibly arousing.

He pulled away and quickly pulled on a rubber. "Roll over." She complied eagerly. The missing pressure of the cherries had left her aching and incomplete.

Dane moved behind her and pushed her onto her elbows so she was tipped up to him, wide and bare. "When you bent over in the living room to show me your sweet ass, I knew I had to take you like this."

"Hurry, Dane." She was already quivering in anticipation. He glided into her with one smooth stroke and she groaned.

"Too deep?" he asked anxiously.

"No, perfect."

"Absolutely perfect," he agreed and began sliding in and out of her. He reached around and stroked her clit and she contracted around his cock, crying his name. "There, a little one to take the edge off, baby. Now you can enjoy the big one."

She shuddered into a gold-lace pillow and tried to ease herself off him. "Too much," she groaned. She wasn't used to the vulnerability of that position.

He held her tight. "Never too much. Not with me."

He curved over her and nipped her shoulder. "I'll take you places you've never been. I'll play with your tits and pussy during the day and fuck you during the night. You'll wake up coming with me inside you and beg me not to stop."

"More, more," she chanted, his words entrancing her and calming her apprehension. He complied eagerly and pounded into her until her world constricted to his big hot body wrapped around her and inside her.

"My sweet dancer, so sexy. You drive me crazy." He broke off into a groan and worked both her breasts with one hand. "Come now, Keeley." He squeezed her nipples with his strong fingers and pinched her clit hard.

She bucked on him as he milked her orgasm, his cock jolting her as his balls bounced on her ass. Time slowed as she screamed her ecstasy into the pillow.

He pulled her upright so she sat on his lap. "Dance on me, baby. Give me the best lap dance ever."

She was too wrung-out to move well but that didn't matter to him. She linked her arms behind his neck and encouraged him to fondle her as she'd never let a club client do. "Touch me, Dane."

He groaned and bit her neck, his hands roaming from her tits to her pussy, just like he'd promised. "Beautiful Keeley." His thrusts quickened, his breath hot on her skin. "Never saw a dancer like you before. Even better than my dreams. Make me come, baby."

She clamped down hard on his cock and ground her ass into him. He grunted and tensed, bellowing her name as his cock erupted in the next instant. She rode him hard, wanting to wring out his every last drop.

He finally panted to a halt and eased onto the

mattress, pulling her into his arms. She snuggled into his chest, content and happy.

He sighed in satisfaction. "Oh, Keeley, you would have made a fortune as a dancer."

She gave a hidden smile. "Thank you." Actually, she *had* earned a ton of money, even without any full-contact stuff. Too bad her CPA degree had cost a fortune, but without it, she wouldn't have met Dane. Lying in his arms, she knew it had been worth it.

11

"OKAY, KEELEY, if you think this'll help, I'll give it a go." Dane crossed his arms over his chest and leaned on the edge of the desk.

She stood in front of the desk and held her palms up, several brightly colored bracelets sliding down her forearms. "I know you like Glenn and he's been one of Binky's best guys, but we still don't have any more information on his wife threatening to divorce him because of his money problems. I tried talking to his assistant, but she either doesn't know or won't say anything."

"Would you say anything about me if your replacement came chatting you up?" He already knew the answer. Keeley was fiercely loyal.

"You know I wouldn't." Her green eyes softened momentarily but then she gave him a wry smile. "Glenn's expecting you, so no more stalling. I'll go over Charlie's newest list of transactions while you're gone."

Dane straightened and sighed. "Yes, ma'am." He brushed her shoulder as he passed her, always eager to steal a touch however he could. He found Glenn in his office.

"Dane, come in. Have a seat." Glenn gestured to the comfortable chair across from him.

"Thanks. I wanted to ask you…" Dane trailed off. Ask him what? If his wife had filed for divorce yet? If he'd declared bankruptcy? If he'd embezzled money?

Glenn cocked his head. "Ask me what?"

Time to try again. "I wanted to get some feedback from you on how I'm doing in my orientation. Binky mentioned you were eager to start your retirement." He felt bad that Glenn wouldn't be starting his retirement as soon as the older man had planned.

"Huh." At Dane's lifted eyebrow, Glenn elaborated, "You're doing fine. It's only that I've got too much on my plate to look forward to retirement right now."

"Really?" Dane assumed what he hoped was a politely interested expression, kind of like a shrink or pastor.

Now that someone was listening, Glenn opened the floodgates. "My mother has lived with my wife and me since she fell at her home several months ago. She's eighty and what you might call a real pistol." Dane mentally translated that as a cranky old broad. "Mom and my wife have never gotten along well, and well, you could say there's a bit of tension at home."

"I see." Dane nodded encouragingly. "Two women, one house."

"Exactly!" The older man heaved a sigh. "So I found a really nice assisted-living senior apartment—a real four-star place. But in order to get the entrance fee, my mother's house has to sell, and this real estate market has been on the slow side. By the time we fixed up the old place, we'd missed the best of the market, so I'm hoping we can sell it this spring."

Talk about motive. "And if you don't have the entrance fee?"

"We lose the apartment and go back to the bottom of the waiting list."

Dane winched. "Rough."

"You're telling me. My mother called the elder abuse hotline just last week because my wife didn't buy breaded mozzarella cheese sticks at the store. Mom has high cholesterol, you see," Glenn finished apologetically.

"And your other investments?" Dane probed delicately.

Glenn snorted. "I have one kid in med school, one in law school, and one finishing at Chicago University. Let's just say my cash is a bit tapped out."

The two men heaved matching sighs—Glenn's obviously as he thought of difficult mothers and tuition bills and Dane's as he thought of how Glenn had motive, means and opportunity. He sincerely hoped it wasn't the current controller, but maybe he'd cracked under family pressure. That was often the worst kind.

KEELEY UNLOCKED the door to her apartment, juggling her overnight bag and laptop case full of audit files. Staying over at Dane's was fun but definitely not restful, and she was fighting off a bit of a spring cold.

He'd been understanding about her need to stay at her place for a day or two and catch up on things. It wasn't so much that she was dying to dust and go grocery shopping, but she needed a bit of a breather from Dane's distracting, sexy presence. All he had to do was look at her and she wanted to take off her clothes.

"Keeley?" A familiar voice called from the living room.

Keeley set down her things and hurried round the corner. "Lacey?" Her younger sister sat on her futon eating the absolute last chocolate ice cream bar, but she was so glad to see her that she didn't even mind. "What are you doing here?"

Lacey unfolded herself from the futon and gave her sister a big hug. "I have a couple days before I leave for northern Wisconsin. My group is helping rehab homes for people in need. Your landlady let me in after I showed her my driver's license. She didn't think there was much family resemblance."

"Well, Mama was a rolling stone." The sisters shared a knowing laugh. Although their eyes were a similar hazel-green, Lacey had her father's African features and coloring.

"Mom is talking about moving west with her new guy. Says they can get seasonal work at a big resort. Work during the summer and drink and smoke cigarettes all winter. And fight." Lacey shrugged. "Does she ever call you?"

"Nope. Now that you're out of there, I have no reason to stay in touch." Her mother hadn't exactly engendered loving memories. "I like your hair, though." Keeley changed the subject and played with her sister's coffee-colored fluff of twisty curls held back by a black patent-leather headband. "Did you get tired of braids?"

"Yeah, too high-maintenance." Lace gave her an odd look. "What's with your hair?"

Keeley reached up to her head and realized she was still wearing her wig, and worst of all, the stripper clothes. She'd never told Lacey about her stripping career and didn't intend to start now. "This? It's a long story." She tugged off the wig and dragged pins out of her real hair.

Lacey watched her with a jaundiced eye. "That's not really helping."

Keeley's shoulders slumped. She must look like Medusa with snaky-looking hair sticking out all over.

Lacey patted her shoulder. "You look like you've had a long day, and there must be a good reason for you to dress like a hoochie mama."

"Hoochie mama?" Keeley sputtered with laughter.

"Believe me, sis, after growing up the way we did, I am an expert on hoochie clothes."

She gave her sister what she thought was a stern look, but Lacey laughed. Oh, well, she couldn't protect her forever, and the life they'd had growing up was a quick way to burst anyone's bubble. "This is a huge secret, but I'm working as a bimbo secretary to do a covert audit at a large financial company."

"Undercover accountant work—how cool is that?" Lacey finally looked impressed with her big sister's career choice. "Now all you need is some way-sexy sidekick and you're all set."

Keeley gave her a weak smile and changed the subject. "Let me hop into the shower and put on some sweatpants. I swear, all this spandex is making me feel like a sausage about to pop open on the grill."

"Mmm." Lacey rubbed her flat nineteen-year-old stomach. No spandex needed for her. "I could go for a Chicago-style dog about now."

"Sounds good. We'll go for dinner at the hot-dog stand." Overcome with happiness at the unexpected visit, she pulled Lacey into a hug. "I'm glad you're here."

"Me, too." Lacey hugged her back. "And you know I have to check on you—make sure you're not getting into trouble," she teased.

"Check on me? Excuse me, little miss, but I am ten

years older than you and don't need any checking on."
Keeley gave Lacey her best haughty look, but wasn't
surprised when her sister rolled her eyes.

"Everybody needs someone to check on them. Especially when they don't think they need anybody."

"Huh?" Keeley hadn't quite followed all those
pronouns.

"Oh, go take your shower." Lacey shooed her down
the hall, and Keeley was only too glad to comply. If
she'd understood her sister right, Lacey was saying
Keeley needed somebody, and Keeley wasn't sure she
liked that idea. Needing somebody was fine as long as
they were willing to be needed, but Dane was only a
temporary need-ee.

DANE FOUND HIMSELF standing in front of Keeley's
apartment Friday night. She had looked so tired, he
wanted to check on her and make sure she was okay. No
wonder she was getting sick. Long days at work and
long nights in bed didn't add up to much rest.

He hadn't expected anyone but Keeley to answer the
door when he knocked, so the young girl answering the
door surprised him. "Um, hi. I'm looking for Keeley.
Does she live here?"

"Uh-huh." She narrowed her green eyes at him, her full
lips pressed into a line as she eyeballed his navy-blue silk
button-down shirt and khakis. "And who might you be?"

Dane introduced himself and explained that they
were working together on a project. That didn't seem
to impress her, so he told her the rest of it. "Keeley and
I are also seeing each other."

"Really?" Her eyes widened. "Figures, she never

mentioned anything…that girl is so tight-lipped. I'm Lacey, Keeley's sister. Hold on." She left him at the door and dashed along the hall.

Keeley's sister? Keeley had never mentioned a sister before, not once. He'd blathered all about his family, his childhood, but she'd never said a word about hers.

Dane sighed and stepped inside the apartment, now that he knew he had the right place. Maybe Lacey lived here and that's why Keeley had never invited him over. He certainly didn't want to set a bad example for anyone.

He turned the corner and his eyes widened. He'd been expecting tan, brown and cream, the colors Keeley had worn as an accountant. But this living room was pure Cherry, bright and bold and cheerful. The futon had a bright red cover with a wide purple ottoman in front. Under it all was a shaggy white area rug with definite possibilities for rolling around naked on it, like a bearskin rug.

He dragged his mind away from that and examined the walls. They were covered in art posters of dancers— the Degas ballerina, one of those Russian-looking ballet guys leaping around and the cancan dancers by Toulouse-Lautrec.

Dane thought her Cherry persona was all an act for the sake of their audit, but maybe it *was* Keeley deep down. This was not the living room of a beige-wearing accountant. Who was Keeley, anyway?

"Here we are!" her sister trilled cheerfully as she shoved Keeley along in front of her.

Keeley looked adorable in a plain black T-shirt and midcalf black exercise pants, her wet hair in ropes on her shoulders. She'd taken off her fake eyelashes and all of her makeup, and he noticed again how beautiful her skin was, clear and smooth as a peach. And how pretty her lips were, even though they were now pressed together in annoyance because he'd dropped in without calling. "Dane, I thought we were going to take a couple days off."

"I was in the neighborhood?" He looked at her sheepishly.

She put her hands on her hips. "Oh, yeah? What brings you to Ukrainian Village?"

"I had a taste for Ukrainian food?" Like he had any idea what that consisted of. "You know, dumplings, sausages…"

Lacey burst into giggles. "Keel, cut the poor man a break."

Dane gave Keeley his best smile and she visibly softened. Thank you, dimples. He'd never thought they were much of anything until Keeley had stuck her tongue in them.

"If you want to kiss him hello or something, I can turn my back," Lacey offered, not quite sarcastically, but close.

"Not necessary," Dane answered. The sisters looked disappointed, Keeley hiding her disappointment more quickly. Dane pulled her into his arms, needing to bend for once since she was in bare feet.

He kissed her thoroughly but sweetly, his lips moving over hers. She stood stiffly for a second, but relaxed into his embrace and wrapped her arms around his neck. She responded eagerly to him, her breath coming faster, and he was beginning to respond a little too eagerly than was appropriate for her sister watching. He finished with a single peck and lifted his head.

Lacey stood there wide-eyed. "Wow, that was some

kiss. Were you out of the country or something? When was the last time you saw each other?"

Dane made a big show of checking his watch. "Five o'clock."

Lacey glanced at the clock on the end table. It was six-thirty. "Da-yum," she said, much impressed.

Keeley buried her face in his shoulder in embarrassment and Dane dropped a kiss on her wet hair to hide his own face, not wanting to admit to himself that ninety minutes without Keeley had seemed a week.

"OH, MY GOD, why didn't you tell me you had such a hottie panting after you?" Lacey flopped backward on the old blanket Dane had earlier tossed onto the grass under some trees. "You have your very own sexy sidekick and you never told me!"

"Shhh!" Keeley made sure Dane wasn't returning from the concession stand yet with their dinner. He had invited both of them to a lakefront concert at Millennium Park. Keeley had been reluctant to go without her Cherry getup but Dane and Lacey insisted, Dane pointing out the extremely small possibility of anyone from Bingham Brothers attending a popular rock concert.

Lacey smiled. "Don't worry, it'll take him a while longer. Everyone in the city is here. And I don't see why you wanted me to come with. Hello! Two's company, three's a crowd."

Keeley couldn't admit she needed a chaperone to keep herself from making a fool of herself over Dane. "You're only in town for two days and I want to spend time with you as well."

"Oh-kay," she grumbled but cheered right up. "Don't

worry, you can have him all to yourself again since I'm leaving for Wisconsin Monday."

"Who's going to Wisconsin?" Dane was back, carefully balancing a mountain of food. Lacey leaped up and helped him with it, divvying the goodies.

"I'm going to Wisconsin to rehab homes for the disadvantaged," Lacey told him proudly. "Outside Green Bay. If we get a chance, we'll go for a boat ride and maybe have a fish boil."

"Wonderful! My home state." They beamed at each other, and Keeley felt a bit left out. Dane handed Lacey his drink and pulled out a business card and pen. "My parents don't live too far away. Here's their contact information if you need anything." He scribbled on the card and handed it to Lacey.

She tried handing it back. "No, that's not necessary—they don't even know me."

He shrugged. "Everyone in Wisconsin is friendly—it's a state law. I'll call them later and let them know you might get in touch."

"Oh, well, thanks." Lacey tucked the card into her wallet and started on her hot dog.

Keeley put her hand on his forearm and he smiled at her, covering her hand with his. "Thank you, Dane." She took a bite of her juicy beef sandwich.

"No problem. I always have a couple local contact numbers when I travel. In fact, when we're done here in Chicago, I'll probably be working in Europe for a while."

The beef turned to cardboard in her mouth. She'd known they didn't have a permanent thing going on, but it still hurt to hear it. "Oh, right. Europe."

Lacey must have only heard the last bit of their conversation thanks to the bands warming up, because all she said was. "Europe? Cool. Keeley's never been to Europe before, but she's dying to go. Have you seen all her posters? She wants to see those paintings in Paris and go to a real Russian-style ballet."

Keeley was glad it was getting dark because her face must have been red. Once the audit was finished, Dane wouldn't want her to go to Europe with him. Keeley had been so sure of it that she hadn't bothered applying for a passport.

Dane said, "Your sister probably can't leave all her clients to go to Europe right now. It's difficult to take a vacation when you run your own business."

"Oh, sure." Lacey wiped off her hands. "Hey, I'm gonna move closer so I can hear the band better." She jumped up and left Keeley alone with Dane.

Keeley cleared her throat. "I didn't tell Lacey about your inviting me to London."

"I'm glad you didn't. We should set a good example for her."

She smiled. Her little sister had been exposed to more bad examples than Dane could imagine. "It's nice of you to think of that. She and I have pretty much managed on our own, so she hasn't met a lot of decent men."

"Well, I'm glad you have someone looking out for *you*." He gave an embarrassed chuckle. "I didn't know that you wanted to travel so badly. And all the dance posters. I guess I've been doing most of the talking and not learning anything about you. You don't say much about yourself."

Keeley started to protest his assessment and then realized he was probably right. Her childhood hadn't been anything to brag about, living with a clueless mother who dragged men home in a futile attempt to make herself feel better. And then dancing at the Love Shack, where the customers didn't give a rat's ass about what or who the dancers were. The girls could have been robots for all they cared, except management would have cared if someone threw a drink at a robot. At least the dancers couldn't short out and electrocute someone.

"You're right," she said painfully. "I guess I never thought anyone would be interested." Her mother had certainly not encouraged open communication about deep personal feelings.

"I'm interested. Tell *me*." With his back resting against the tree, Dane pulled her onto his lap, and Keeley told him. The darkness made it easier to spill her guts, as she confessed about living in the trailer park with a biracial baby sister who got teased terribly and cooking mac and cheese in the microwave and sitting terrified and alone on the couch until their mom came home from the convenience store after her shift there ended at 3:00 a.m.

He rubbed her tears away with his big thumb but didn't say anything until she told him about fighting off her mom's boyfriends as a teenager and paying for Lacey's karate classes to get her black belt so she would be strong and not vulnerable.

Then he muttered a string of obscenities aimed at those men who would have harmed her. "Ah, Keeley. You tell me who they are, and I'll drive there and beat the crap out of them."

"What?"

He was deadly serious. "I'll call my brothers Colin

and Adam, and the three of us will drive to Shitburg, Southern Illinois, and teach them that real men don't mess with little girls."

"Oh, Dane. That's the nicest thing anyone's ever offered to do for me."

"Then you haven't been around the right people, sweetheart." He kissed her forehead.

"I suppose I haven't. That job I had, the one that helped put me through school…" She took a deep breath, ready to explain the origins of her Bingham Brothers wardrobe.

"Keeley! Dane!" Lacey burst back into their intimate dark cocoon, stopping when she saw Keeley sitting on his lap. "Oh, sorry, sis. I ran into some of my friends from the rehab trip and they have an extra ticket for a midnight cruise of Lake Michigan. Do you mind if I go? I've never been on the lake before."

"I don't know, Lacey. You're not familiar with the city and you might have a hard time finding a cab," she fretted.

Lacey put her hands on her hips. "I'm not a baby anymore, and I do have that black belt in karate you paid for. Gimme a break."

Dane intervened before Keeley could give her sister a much-needed attitude adjustment. "Hey, how about you meet your sister and me at my place? It's not too far from here and every cabbie in the city knows the building. You and Keeley can have my guest room for the night."

Lacey gave Keeley what might have looked like a smirk in better light. "That okay, big sis?"

"Fine." They were ganging up on her anyway. Dane moved her off his lap and gave Lacey his address and what looked like a twenty for cab fare. Lace gave her a cheery wave and trotted off to meet her friends.

Just then, the band started with a screech—the electric guitars as well as the lead singer. After a few seconds, Keeley mostly tuned it out, something she'd learned to do at the club. Dane's expression grew more and more pained until she couldn't help laughing. "Not enjoying this?"

He shook his head. "No, and you're talking to a guy who grew up on heavy-metal bands. These guys are just rust."

"They're the front band. They'll do a set before the main attraction."

"If you're still not feeling good, we could go to my place and watch a movie," he offered, obviously hoping to escape the awful music.

"My sister could come home anytime," she warned him.

He helped her to her feet and stood. "Keel, I've had a long week, too. We won't do anything you'd be embarrassed for your sister to walk in on. I accidentally dropped in on my sister and her fiancé once, and…" He shuddered. "Not something I care to repeat."

"Poor Dane," she cooed, taking his hand. "Hopefully I've helped you put that out of your mind."

He raised their interlaced fingers to his mouth and kissed them. "You have indeed."

KEELEY FLIPPED ON Dane's enormous flat-screen television. You practically needed an electronic engineering degree to run the thing, but she managed to find some good channels.

"Dane, the new James Bond movie is playing on pay-per-view. I've only seen the trailer—do you want to watch it?"

He was in the kitchen fixing some snacks and called, "Bond, huh? Good choice."

"Bond it is." Keeley wandered back into the ultra-modern kitchen and leaned on the chilly granite countertop. "Do you need any help?"

"Making microwave popcorn?" He slanted a grin at her while pulling out the fancy sliding pantry shelves. "You are looking at the king of microwave popcorn. What else is there to eat when you're alone in a hotel room watching any movie you can find?" He popped a bag in and pressed a couple buttons.

"Sounds lonely," she commented without thinking.

He shrugged, his wide shoulders to her as he filled a couple glasses with ice. Like she was one to talk. She was used to loneliness. Her dad had left before she was born, her mom had been permanently checked out mentally, and the only person she could count on was her little Lacey.

Not so little anymore, though, with her own college education and bright future ahead of her. Lacey would leave her, and it was right for her to do that. Keeley would be the mama bird kicking her baby out of the nest so she could try her wings and soar.

She sighed hard enough to ruffle Dane's hair across the room. He turned to her. "Hey, what's up? That sounded sad."

"Just thinking about Lacey going off on her own."

"To Wisconsin? Don't worry, it's pretty tame there. That's why I left." He laughed.

"No, I mean in general. We have our own lives now and she doesn't need me anymore."

He frowned. "Of course she still needs you. Maybe

not for a babysitter, but she'll always need you. My brother and sister and I all need each other and I doubt that will change."

"You sure?"

"Absolutely. And when Lacey's not around, you must have quite an active social life."

She shrugged. "I have the world's largest collection of single-serving frozen dinners. Aside from a client lunch or dinner with Sugar, it's me and the microwave for company."

"Now I have a hard time believing that, Keeley." He moved closer to her and brushed a strand of hair away from her face. "Are all the men in Chicago blithering idiots? Do none of them see how beautiful you are? What a nice person you are?"

"That's sweet of you, but I've been too busy with school and starting my accounting practice."

He cupped her chin and tilted her face up to his. "Their loss is my gain." He bent and kissed her, softly, sweetly. She returned his kiss, but all the time knowing he would soon be off to Europe or wherever and his kisses would only be a memory.

Some of her ambivalence must have come through in her response because he broke off the kiss. "What's wrong?" he whispered against her lips.

She pulled away. "Um, nothing. I think the popcorn's starting to burn." It wasn't.

"What?" He crossed to the microwave in two big strides and shut it off, checking the popcorn. "No, I think we're good. What do you want to drink?"

Glad for something to do, Keeley opened the stainless-steel fridge. Nothing much in there but chip dip and several bottles of beer. "Is that a German import? I've never heard of it."

"Wisconsin import," he called. "The brewery's not too far from where I grew up."

"Cool." She shifted the bottles to see the different varieties and stifled a laugh. The pale beer had an interesting name. She grabbed two bottles and closed the fridge.

"What did you find?" He came toward her with a big bowl of popcorn.

She wiggled the bottles at him. "This beer is called 'Honey Weiss.' Sounds sweet and tasty to me. Like you, Mr. Weiss."

He started to flush. "Yeah, um, they only make that in spring and summer. 'Weiss' is the German word for 'white,' because it's a pale ale."

"Are you my honey, Weiss?"

Now the tips of his ears reddened, but he set the bowl on the counter. "Put down the beer bottles, my sweet Keeley."

When she waved them teasingly, he plucked them from her hands and set them on the table. "Do you *want* me to be your honey?" He yanked her close, pinning her wrists behind her with one strong hand. He nibbled her neck, making her arch her pelvis against him. "Sweet and sticky all over you?"

"Yes," she moaned. "But my sister…"

"She'll be on the lake until midnight and the doorman will call first anyway. I'll go get something from the bathroom."

She took a deep breath. "No, Dane. I'm on birth control and tested." She didn't want him to go anywhere. "We're both okay, right?"

"I'm healthy, and I haven't been with anyone in a while." He bit her ear. "That, combined with how damn sexy you are, almost made my balls fall off until you let me make love to you."

Her eyes flew open. Make love? He was probably trying to be romantic.

His other hand slipped under her shirt, unerringly finding her nipple. "I'll do whatever you want, Keeley. You know that. You've got me twisted up in knots. When you're near me, I can't keep my hands off you." He teased and pinched her nipple. "When we're apart, I wonder if you're thinking about me, too." He shuddered in desire. "The thought of making love to you, being *in* you without any barrier…I'd do anything for that."

Keeley was about to come just from his sexy words. "Now, Dane. Let's make love—" her tongue stumbled across the unfamiliar words "—without anything between us."

He let go of her and stripped off his clothes until he stood naked and aroused, raw and earthy in the kitchen's gleaming sterility.

She followed his example, the sight of his work-hardened muscles captivating her as usual. He sat on a chair and spread his thighs, his cock pointing up invitingly. Her pussy clenched, wanting to accept that hard, hot invitation.

She walked over to Dane, her mouth suddenly dry with nerves. "Thirsty?" She tipped some beer into his mouth and drank some herself, bending over so her breasts swayed near his face. The beer was light and tasted of honey. "Mmm, sweet."

Dane swallowed a mouthful and took the bottle from

her. "Not as sweet as you." Instead of taking another drink, he poured the icy beer over her breasts. Keeley gasped, her nipples peaking instantly. She had seen that done with other girls at the club but had not allowed it herself. But there was something elementally lascivious about having a sexy man become drunk off her body as well as beer.

He eagerly lifted his head and licked the rivulets, lapping drops off the tight buds.

Keeley grabbed on to his shoulders, catching her breath as he took another mouthful of beer. Instead of swallowing it, though, he took a mouthful of her.

The cold carbonation fizzed on her sensitive nipple, making her squeal. Dane chuckled in the back of his throat, swallowed and repeated it with her other nipple, sending hot streams of desire to her pussy.

She arched her spine, giving him eager access as he made love to her breasts, pouring and sipping the beer over her until the bottle was empty.

Setting it on the countertop with a clink, he ran both hands over her body as if he couldn't get enough of touching her. "I swear, if the girl on the beer ad looked like you, I would have drunk too much to ever get through school. Cold beer licked off a hot woman." He spread her thighs and dove into her liquid center, teasing and playing with her clit until her legs weakened. He slipped a finger inside her, rotating it slowly. She groaned and shuddered a bit when he caught her G-spot. "You're ready for me, Keeley. Come get me."

She positioned herself over him with each foot on either side of the chair and sank bare inch by delicious bare inch until they fit like a key and lock. They groaned, his cock jerking in time to her own pulsations.

"You're so hot," they both said in unison, and laughed. Without the condom, she could *really* feel him, the fat head indenting sharply to the thick shaft, silky smooth and slick with both their juices.

"Sweet Keeley." His fingers dug into her thighs. "All for me, only for me. Tight and wet. Gonna die if you don't move on me."

She used her strong thighs to lever herself up and down his pole, gasping every time she hit bottom. His balls were tight and warm on her ass, and she was spread wide open. Dane moved his hands around from her breasts and cupped her ass. He spread her even wider, playing with the cleft and dipping lower.

She stopped for a second at the unfamiliar caress, but he coaxed her on. "Relax, you'll like it. Trust me."

She did trust him, so she put her pleasure in his hands and moved even faster, plucking at her clit at the same time. He tensed under her as she brushed his cock with her nail. He swirled his finger in her moisture and gently teased her bottom opening. Keeley moaned at the un-expectedly sharp feeling. Encouraged, he penetrated her there, too.

"Oh, Dane." She was swamped with lust extending from her clit all the way back. She was spread wide open and should have felt vulnerable, but not with him.

"You like it?" he rasped.

She nodded, her head tossing back and forth.

"I love it. I love bad girls. Only a bad girl would let me do this, dance naked for me, let me suck beer off her tits. Are you my bad girl, Keeley?"

"I am, I'm a really bad girl," she cried, caught up with the double penetration of his bare flesh. He swelled even farther inside her, his fingers moving in rhythm with her. He buried his face between her breasts, not saying anything for once, just making several lusty groans. Lightning shot from her clit all the way to her ass. "Oh!"

"Call me *honey* when you come," he groaned. "I wanna hear you talk for once." He sucked her nipple hard into his mouth and she broke apart on top of him, her pussy squeezing on every inch of his long, bare cock.

"Honey, honey, my sweet honey Dane, oh!" He trapped her onto his cock and finger as she chanted his name over and over.

He kissed her open, gasping mouth, rubbing his tongue along hers. "Take my honey, baby." He slammed up and jetted into her, his hot seed bathing and overflowing her as she cried out at the unfamiliar sensation.

He gave one last roar and slumped onto the kitchen chair. She fell onto his chest and stuck. They were a mess, covered in beer, sweat and sex juices. Keeley kissed the racing pulse at the base of his throat and laughed. "That's how to enjoy a Wisconsin Honey Weiss."

He sighed in satisfaction. "That's how to enjoy my honey, Keeley."

12

KEELEY RECLINED against Dane on his huge leather couch. They were both showered and fully dressed in anticipation of Lacey's return and had polished off a second bowl of popcorn. Keeley was in a mellow mood now and hadn't wanted to watch the tension-packed James Bond flick. She was idly flipping channels instead. "Oh, look, Dane. *G.I. Blues* is playing. I've seen practically every Elvis movie ever made."

Dane looked up briefly at the TV and returned to nuzzling her neck. "Oh, yeah. This is the one set in Germany." Elvis began to sing "Wooden Heart," one of his more popular songs that mixed German and English. "Hmm. He actually doesn't have a bad accent."

"I've always thought that was a dumb title. A wooden heart? Sounds like a carved knickknack you'd find in one of those gift shops with all the cuckoo clocks."

"You haven't seen German knickknacks 'til you've come to Wisconsin. Besides, I think the girl in the movie is being wooden, or cold to him, or something. Not like you." He slipped his hand under her shirt to caress her belly, but for once, Keeley wasn't paying attention to his touch.

A wooden heart. She sometimes felt she was cut off from people, a bit cold. Oh, sure, she had loved her mother once upon a time, but her negligence and indifference had pretty much killed any affection. Lacey, though. She loved Lacey with all her heart and always had. But sisters aside, she'd never loved a man, never been in love. She sympathized with the girl in the movie. After all, a wooden heart was not easily broken.

When Elvis came to the German refrain, Dane started singing along in a pleasing baritone voice. Elvis stopped, but Dane continued, singing a couple more verses softly into her ear.

Keeley could understand a few words from its similarity to English, but missed almost all of it. "Dane, I didn't know you could sing like that."

He shrugged, his ears turning pink. "My mom's mother was born in Germany and my dad's side of the family was Swiss, so our family were regular members of the local German heritage club."

"So you speak it?" He nodded. "What do the words say?"

"The first verse Elvis sings is about how he has to leave his girl to go find his fortune but he'll come back again for her."

"And what were the verses you sang?"

"Oh, more of the same." He turned back to the TV, settling her between his thighs. "Let's see what Elvis is going to do now."

"Probably dance and sing—surprise, surprise." Now she was intrigued. "Tell me what you sang to me."

"I told you—more of the same."

"Tell me." She rolled over to face him. "Or I'll tickle it out of you."

"Go ahead." He spread his arms wide. "Not gonna work."

"Oh, yeah?" She did her best, tickling his neck and sides, even under the arms of his T-shirt. He smiled smugly at her, but it was obvious she wasn't bothering him at all. "Why aren't you ticklish?"

He finally laughed. "I have a brother, a sister and about seventeen cousins. I learned real quick to not be ticklish."

"Oh."

"How about you, Keeley? Do you have any deep, dark secrets I can tickle out of you?" He crept his fingers up her ribs, making her giggle.

"Nope."

"Are ya sure?" He increased the pressure and speed, running his hands all over her body. She laughed so hard she lost her breath, unable to tell him anything. In a last-ditch effort to get away, she rolled off the couch onto the rug. He followed, catching his weight on his arms before he landed on her. "You okay, sweetheart? I didn't mean for you to do that."

"I'm fine." She smiled at him, eager to drop the subject of deep, dark secrets.

"You're more than fine." He settled his body over hers. "Our tickling match does have its advantages." He bent his head to kiss her, but the condo buzzer rang.

"Oh, Dane, it's probably my sister." She gave him a quick hug and he stood and helped her to her feet. He went over to the intercom and the doorman announced they had a Miss Lacey Davis come to visit and should he send her up.

. Lacey must have taken the receiver away from the doorman because her cheerful voice rang out. "Get dressed, y'all, cuz I'm coming!"

Keeley pressed her hands against her burning cheeks and Dane roared with laughter. "Get your butt up here and stop embarrassing your sister—she's red as a beet."

"We *are* dressed, you little snot!" Keeley called. Lacey laughed uproariously and hung up.

"Good thing she didn't get here earlier, huh?" Dane wiggled his blond brows suggestively, starting another blush for her.

"Stop it!" She swatted him in the arm, her hand bouncing harmlessly off his bicep. "You're as bad as she is."

"Oh, come on, Keeley." He caught her hand and kissed it. "We're just kidding you because we love you." He went to open the door for her sister, leaving Keeley shell-shocked in the middle of the luxurious foyer.

Had Dane even realized what he said? Did it even mean anything? After all, he had lumped himself in with her sister in the whole "love" verb.

He ushered her sister in as an honored guest, chatting with her and giving her the grand tour. Keeley followed behind them, watching Dane's indulgent expression as small-town Lacey goggled over his condo. He actually liked her sister and wasn't making nice with her to please Keeley.

Just then, Dane gave Keeley a smile of such sweetness that her own wooden heart cracked right down the middle. All of a sudden, Lacey wasn't the only person Keeley loved. Now there was a second. Dane Weiss.

And Keeley just knew she would wind up with some very painful splinters.

KEELEY CAME OUT from her apartment kitchen where she'd been packing some nonperishable snacks for Lacey to eat while on the rehab job site. "Here's some of those chewy granola bars, some trail mix, yellow and red apples, raisins and cheese crackers."

"Good grief, Keel, I'm remodeling houses, not climbing Mount Everest. But thanks."

"You're welcome. Now here's some money for that fish boil or boat ride you were talking about." Keeley tucked a few twenties and fifties into a zipper pocket on her sister's backpack.

Lacey saw one of the fifties and her eyes widened. "I don't want to take all your money on you. Unless Dane gave it to you?"

"No, this is *my* money, not his. I'm not taking any money from Dane. I'm making a bundle on this consulting job and I don't need any man to give me anything."

"Okay, geez, sorry." Lacey held up her hands in placation. Her expression turned sly. "So does that mean you're only using him for sex?"

"Lacey Jo Davis! You are the most, the absolutely most outrageous girl…" Keeley sputtered to a stop while Lacey fell onto the futon laughing.

"Look at you blush. I didn't think anything made you blush—and now a man does? Must be some hot lovin' going on."

Keeley squawked in protest. "We only started seeing

each other a few weeks ago. Honestly, Lacey, I don't know how you get these ideas."

Her sister rolled her eyes. "Oh, I don't know—cuz he looks at you like he just walked out of the Sahara and you're an ice cream sundae?"

"He does not."

"Does to."

"Does not."

"Does to, does to, does to, and you know it, cuz you look at him the same way."

Keeley assumed a haughty expression. "I'm sure I don't know what you're talking about. I had so hoped that once you started college, you would grow in wisdom—" She broke off into a shriek as Lacey tickled her around the waist.

"You're full of more bull than Dane's family's farm. Don't lie to me—are you in luuuuve?"

Keeley stiffened. "Stop."

Her serious tone made Lacey's eyes widen. "Oh, my God—you *are* in love! Does he know that? I'm sure he loves you, too. You've never been in love before. Wow, are you gonna move in together? Or even get married?"

"Lacey, please." Keeley sat cross-legged on the flokati rug. "Dane and I, well, things are complicated. We're in the middle of that tricky audit and after that, he wants to leave for Europe to do some work over there." She gave what had to be a weak smile at Lacey, whose expression was growing stormier and stormier as she listened. "Anyway, I have my clients to keep me busy, and of course you. You're my top priority."

"Bullshit!" Lacey exploded. "Your dumb-ass clients? Haven't they ever heard of e-mail and file attachments?

And me? I live three hundred miles away and eat, sleep and breathe college. I love you more than anybody, sis, but I will not let you use me as an excuse for wimping out on this great thing you have with Dane."

"I am not using you as an excuse!" The accusation stung. Lacey pursed her lips but didn't say anything. "Am I?" Her sister nodded. "I'm not meaning to."

"Now that you know, cut it out. Tell the man how you feel." Lacey shook her curly head. "If I had such a hot, nice, sweet guy panting after me, I'd be all over him like white on rice."

"You would, would you? And has a guy like that come along for you?" Keeley hoped not. Lacey still had three years of college to go.

"Nope, not yet." She laughed. "And you can bet I'll be the pickiest chick you ever met. No second-stringers for me."

"And Dane's the starting quarterback," Keeley said dreamily.

Lacey giggled. "He's built more like an offensive linesman, sugar, but to each her own. Now, go tackle that man and bring him to his knees."

KEELEY STRODE through the office first thing Monday morning. She'd just finished looking over Glenn's accounts and he looked clean. According to the P.I.'s report and Dane's latest chat with the older man, his mother's house had sold and she was safely ensconced in her new apartment. Dane said Glenn was practically giddy with relief.

Keeley, on the other hand, wasn't giddy about her upcoming meeting. Mrs. Hobson had e-mailed her

Friday to set up a meeting to "help Cherry learn more about the Bingham Brothers corporate culture." More like take her to task for her clothing and rather obvious affair with her boss.

Keeley couldn't have picked a better pair of shoes for her little tête-à-tête with Charlie's executive assistant. The four-inch clear Lucite heels actually had little embedded colored lights that flashed with every step. They were tacky even for a stripper, unthinkable for an environment such as this one.

Which was probably why Amanda Hobson had been insistent on seeing her. Charlie Bingham had probably ordered the older lady to talk some sense into her about what was appropriate and what wasn't. Keeley had no intention of changing her look but wanted the chance to snoop about what Charlie was up to.

Keeley knocked on the doorjamb and entered Mrs. Hobson's open office. "Hiya, Mrs. H. How're ya doin'?" If she'd had gum she would have cracked it.

Mrs. H. looked up from her computer and visibly blanched. Keeley didn't blame her and had actually avoided looking in the mirror that morning herself. Today she was wearing a leopard-print skirt along with a gold lamé top that would have seemed cheesy on a 1970s disco dancer. The skirt was longer than her usual Bingham Brothers attire but had a slit in the back going up into outer space.

"Miss…Smith." Mrs. Hobson was looking at her skirt as if it were a real leopard about to pounce on her. She shook herself and recovered slightly. "Please, sit. If you can, in that skirt," she muttered.

Keeley perked up her ears and sat. A sarcastic side, huh? "Oh, please, call me Cherry. Everyone does."

"Fine. Cherry."

Keeley looked at a few framed photos of old ladies on Mrs. Hobson's desk while she waited for her to offer her first name in return, but decided she'd be waiting forever. "What did you want to see me about?" she asked, purposely dangling her question.

"Cherry, Mr. Bingham asked me to talk to you about your work attire."

"Which Mr. Bingham? Charlie? Can't be Binky, because I ran into the old sweetie yesterday and he told me how I brightened up the place."

Mrs. Hobson's mouth disappeared into a thin line, either at her calling the *über*-bosses by their first names or at Binky's well-known penchant for déclassé dames such as herself. "The elder Mr. Bingham doesn't come to the office regularly, so perhaps he is not acquainted with what we consider business wear."

"Ah." Keeley nodded and tried to look stupid. "I haven't been wearing pants or jeans or anything casual like that."

Mrs. Hobson raised an eyebrow and tried a different tack. "Did you work for Mr. Weiss before coming here? I know he made a special request to bring you aboard."

Hmm, nosy now? "Mutual friends introduced us, I was looking for a job and he hired me."

"Did you formerly work in the entertainment field, dear? You have quite the theatrical flair."

"Thank you." Keeley smiled, not answering her question, which was hitting too close to the mark.

The older lady pursed her lips. "Mr. Weiss has been going through the accounts. Has he mentioned why?"

Keeley shrugged but wondered about her asking. "I guess that's part of his job. I don't know too much about this finance stuff. It's not like I'm an accountant or anything." She couldn't resist that inside joke.

"Oh, I think you know plenty about money." Her thin lips tightened even further.

"What?" Had she blown her cover already? Dane was not going to be happy. But how? "The only thing I know about money is that having more is better than having less."

Mrs. Hobson nodded smugly. "I could tell. You can always tell, with girls like you."

Ouch. "Whaddya mean, girls like me?" Keeley let some of her own anger spill into her voice. This old troll was why Keeley didn't go around telling people how she'd worked her way through school.

"It's bad for office morale when employees are over-familiar with their employers. Lives can be ruined for much less."

Keeley thought this was a bit over-the-top but was intrigued. "What do you mean?"

Mrs. Hobson stared at her. "Families torn apart, children hurt."

"But Dane isn't married, and he doesn't have any children." Was the older lady batty?

"That's what you're aiming for, isn't it? Dane Weiss will never marry you, you know. They never do."

"Mrs. Hobson, I'm not interested in marrying Dane." That wasn't quite true. She had thought about it a couple times, the way you thought about being an astronaut or winning the lottery.

She gave an unladylike snort, obviously seeing through Keeley. "Right. Don't listen to me. You can screw your boss six ways to Sunday and see how far it gets you. If I were you, I'd keep my résumé updated. Once he's tired of you, you're history." She pointedly turned back to her computer.

Keeley blinked in surprise and let herself out. That bit of friendly advice had been about the most *unfriendly* advice she'd ever received, and she'd had plenty of work confrontations at the strip club. Mrs. Hobson had an ax to grind somewhere in her past. Had she slept with a boss and had the roof fall in on her head?

She turned the corner into her own office and found just the person to ask. Binky Bingham sat across from Dane, both men standing when she came in. Dane introduced them in a low voice, using her real name. The private investigator had come through that morning and swept for surveillance, installing a few countermeasures of his own.

"Have we ever met, my dear? You seem terribly familiar." Binky eyed her avidly, her outlandish outfit like bacon in front of a dog.

Keeley plastered a smile on her face. Binky very well could have seen her act at the Love Shack. Good thing she wasn't naked with a can of whipped cream, or he would have pegged her for sure. "We've never met, although Sugar speaks very highly of you."

Her attempt at distraction worked. His wrinkly face lit up at the mention of her. "Ah, Sugar." He lapsed into a reverie, obviously replaying his mental highlights film, of Sugar only, she hoped.

Dane beckoned her to his side. "What's up?" he whispered. "You've got that scowl that tells me you're thinking hard about something."

"I don't scowl," she whispered back.

"Yeah, you do." He ran a finger between her brows. "Right here, it gets all furrowed."

"Furrowed?" She felt for herself. Ugh, he meant wrinkled.

"It's a farm word. So tell me what you're thinking."

"I need to know more about Mrs. Hobson," she said under her breath. "What do you know about her?"

"She's been Charlie's secretary forever, even worked for his dad. But I don't know much more than that. You'll have to ask Binky."

"Mr. Bingham." She bent over to get his attention, and parts of her did the job. She snapped her fingers in front of her breasts and pointed to her face.

Dane coughed to cover a laugh, but Keeley continued, "Mr. Bingham, I need to know more about Mrs. Hobson."

That really got his attention. "Mrs. Hobson? Why?"

Did he sound cagey, or was it just her? She looked over at Dane, who wore a puzzled expression. "Does she have any reason to want to hurt this company?"

Dane snorted. "Her? Come on, Keeley."

She ignored him. "Tell me, Mr. Bingham. She was pretty angry underneath her prim facade."

Binky sighed, his shoulders slumping. "I can't think it's possible, but yes."

She sat next to him. "Go on."

"Amanda Hobson worked for my son Charles Andrew the Fifth, whom we called Quint. Quint was a wonderful boy." The older man stared off into space and swallowed hard but continued, "Wonderful, but reckless. Reckless in his sports—he would ride the wildest horse, ski the tallest mountain, swim the roughest seas.

"After Charlie was born, I begged him to ease up. He had nothing to prove." He turned to smile at Keeley. "If he were a young man today, he would be one of those professional 'extreme' athletes and not have a thing to do with Bingham Brothers. But that wasn't how it worked thirty years ago. I told Quint to come on board or I would cut off his money."

Keeley nodded. Hard to be a slacker rich boy without any dough. Poor slackers didn't have much fun.

"So Quint moped around the offices until he hired Amanda. After that, he was happy here, productive, and going home to his wife, Julia, and Charlie at night. And if he chose to take his secretary on business trips, who were we to object?"

"Tax-deductible, too," Keeley murmured. Quint sounded like a real jerk. Dane caught her eye and shook his head. She subsided grudgingly, letting Binky finish the story to which they all could guess the ending.

"Quint came to me about a year later and told me he was going to leave his wife for Amanda. We fought terribly, especially since my own secretary had overhead Amanda bragging about how much money she would have once she married Quint. Apparently Amanda had developed a taste for the jet-set life thanks to my son. Finally he agreed to wait six months to try to work things out with Julia for Charlie's sake. I suppose you could say I won, but I'm not so sure. I had Amanda transferred into the accounting department to get her away from him."

Keeley whipped her head around, meeting Dane's surprised look. Accounting, huh?

"Quint took his family to Switzerland for Christmas, and…" Binky sighed. "He hit a patch of ice on the black diamond run and went headfirst into a tree. Killed instantly."

Keeley winced and patted Binky's hand. "I'm so sorry."

He grasped her fingers, nothing but sincerity shining from his eyes. "It was a long time ago, my dear. I've had decades to come to terms with it."

Sure he had. Nobody ever got over losing a kid.

"Binky, I'm sorry, too," Dane's voice rumbled across the desk.

Keeley was turning the possibilities over in her mind. "So she was transferred away from her married lover, who returned to his family and had a tragic accident before she could win him back, thereby losing him forever."

The men stared at her, obviously not considering the situation from a female point of view. Keeley almost felt sorry for the foolish girl Amanda Hobson had been to pin Quint Bingham as her meal ticket out of the typing pool. Almost sorry, but not quite.

"Even so, she's just a secretary. She wouldn't have the foggiest idea how to steal from the company's trust funds."

She turned on Dane. "Like I'm *just* a secretary? I've found so many gaps in the safeguards, I could take a billion dollars and be in Brazil before you even blinked."

Binky looked nervously at Dane. She sighed. "No, I am not going to steal your money and become a fugitive, Binky. But do *not* underestimate her because she's an older woman. She is a woman who lost forever the man she loved because of *you,* Binky." She pointed at him. "What better way to have her revenge than to wreck your company and put your grandson in jail?"

CHARLIE BINGHAM poked his head out of his office. His executive assistant was whispering into her cell phone, her back turned to him.

"Yes, I already told you the name. I don't care if you think it's fake or not—just find out about her. Get back to me ASAP." She flipped the phone shut and muttered a word that quite frankly shocked him.

He cleared his throat. "Mrs. Hobson?"

She spun to face him, the unusually harsh lines of her face settling into a cheerful expression. "Yes, Mr. Bingham?"

"Well, yes. Um, how did your chat with Mr. Weiss's assistant go?"

"Ah, yes, Cherry." Her nostrils flared, as if she'd smelled something bad. "I tried my best, but she insists on being totally inappropriate for our office. You may have to demand that Mr. Weiss replace her."

Charlie successfully choked down his laughter. Him demand anything of Dane? No, thanks, he liked having all his limbs attached. "Regretfully, Cherry was a condition of Mr. Weiss's employment arrangement with my grandfather. Mr. Weiss is quite attached to her, so unless something egregious comes up, I'm afraid Cherry stays on."

"Something egregious?"

"Obviously if she were caught embezzling from the client accounts, we could fire her, although I don't believe she has enough brains to steal a box of paper clips." Charlie laughed at the idea of the redheaded bimbo embezzling anything, but his assistant didn't see the humor. Oh, well. That was nothing new.

"DO YOU REALLY THINK Mrs. Hobson's the thief?" Dane sank into his desk chair after walking a shaken Binky to his limo. Keeley was sorry to be the bearer of bad news, but Binky was a big boy and knew the high stakes they were playing for.

"A strong possibility. Bob from accounting is clean, and so is Glenn. She's been here long enough to learn everything, she has an accounting background, and she has the motive."

"We'll see."

"Do you want Charlie to be the bad guy? Because I don't think he is, despite some of his cash transactions recently."

"I hate the guy's guts, but Binky doesn't deserve the disgrace." He shrugged. "If he is guilty, I'll do my best to protect Binky from the fallout."

"Fair enough." Keeley held her felt-tip poised above the yellow legal pad. "So what's the common denominator of all the account holders?"

Dane flipped through the pages she'd printed for him. "They're all at least Binky's age, if not older."

"What else?"

"They've all been clients of Bingham Brothers for thirty years or more."

"Okay." Keeley wrote both of those on her pad. "Does Binky know them personally?"

"Most of them, as far as I know. They all would have

been heavy hitters on the elite social scene thirty or forty years ago. Binky's one of the last that's still active in society."

"I can tell." Keeley clicked from one client's file to another on her laptop with her other hand. "Aside from Binky, the rest of them have home health care. This one has five thousand a month to Adult Home Care of Chicago, this one has five thousand a month to Adult Home Care of Chicago."

Dane's blue eyes widened with surprise. "So does this one—only here, for fifty-five hundred."

"To Adult Home Care of Chicago?"

He nodded.

"You look through the papers—I'll check the computer files." She had the software tally the health-care expense category, removing the obvious doctor's office visits and hospital stays. The computer popped up a total amount that made her whistle. She scrolled though the payees. "Dane, Adult Home Care of Chicago supposedly takes care of all but three of these clients."

"Supposedly?" He lifted a brow.

"I'm not sure who's actually using home health care. Can you call Binky?"

He nodded, his face set in an expression she'd never seen, taut and fierce, as if he were going hunting. She shivered, hoping she never saw it directed at her.

He made the call, running over the list of names with Binky, his expression growing even grimmer. After hanging up, he passed her a piece of paper. "These and these—" he pointed at several names "—are living in assisted-living apartments or nursing homes. These other ones have absolutely no need for home health care, and in fact four are on an around-the-world cruise and have not been in Chicago for the past six months."

"I'll check who remains on the list." She quickly found two sets of payments—one to Adult Home Care of Chicago and a second to different home-care agencies for varying amounts—probably the legitimate expense. She stared at Dane. "Adult Home Care of Chicago—it's the only common denominator. Each client is being billed between fifty and seventy-five thousand dollars a year for likely nonexistent services."

"And with the sizes of the trust funds, they wouldn't even question it. The trust administrator would authorize the money—after all, old people have expensive health-care bills."

Keeley did a quick calculation. "Dane, if we assume all those payments are fraudulent, the total amount adds up to between one-point-five and two million dollars a year."

"Oh, my God." Dane looked stricken. "That much? How long has this been going on?"

Keeley wanted to go comfort him but forced herself to search backward for the start of the Adult Home Care payments. "Three years ago. Five million dollars total." It made her stomach flip to say it. "Give or take a couple hundred thousand."

"Give or take a couple hundred thousand?" Dane groaned. "Three years ago is when Binky and the board appointed Charlie CFO. That stupid, greedy bastard! He knew what this would do to Binky if he got caught. How could he?"

"How could he?" Keeley echoed. She jumped to her feet, unable to look any longer at the missing million-dollar-plus figure on her computer screen. Her tacky heels sank into the plush carpet as she paced. "Yeah, Dane, *how* could he? It doesn't make sense. How could he get on board and start embezzling right away? He would have had to plan this all months in advance for the ghost payrolling. Is he the type of guy who can do that?"

"Sure, Keeley, he may be a creep, but he's smart, knows his way around finance."

"What does he know about home health? Has Binky ever needed it?"

He shook his head. "No, not even after his heart attack. His regular household help was enough."

"So he's never cared for anyone elderly, never paid the bills for them. Why would he think of home health care?"

"I don't know, Keeley!" Dane threw his hands up in frustration. "Because he's a jackass who wants to screw over his grandfather, his grandfather's company and his grandfather's friends."

"Then he's not the only one. Don't forget Mrs. Hobson, the scorned mistress of Quint Bingham, the one whom Binky sent to *accounting* to get her away from his poor, doomed son?" She stopped and bent to Dane, resting her hands on the table. "She probably cared for an elderly relative and saw how easy it would be to steal that kind of money. After all, the payments are small, regular and reasonable. Get enough victims, and they add up." She slapped the table. "Now I'll bet you anything it's her. Call your P.I. and get him on her."

"You bet me anything?" He looked at her skeptically.

She pointed at her computer screen. "I bet you five million dollars."

He finally smiled. "You're on. But if you lose, I'm

holding you to your bet." He cupped her neck and gave her a quick kiss. "At five dollars a kiss."

"A million kisses? That'll take forever," she half-heartedly protested.

Dane winked at her and flipped open his phone. "Fine with me."

Keeley blinked in shock and fled across the room to her laptop, wondering what in the world he meant.

"HEY, DANE, what's with the goofy smile?" Adam slugged Dane's shoulder as he found him in the neighborhood tavern they both enjoyed.

Dane looked up from where he'd been grinning at his bottle of beer. "Nothing." It would take torture to make him admit to a buddy that his Keeley was sweet as honey and twice as delicious.

Adam dropped into the stool next to him. "Well, it can't be baseball because the Brewers have dropped nine straight, and it can't be the Packers because it's off-season for football. So it must be a wo-mannn." He dragged out the last word teasingly as if they were still in school.

"Nope." Unfortunately, Dane felt the blush creeping up his neck and ears.

His friend guffawed. "Look at you. Red as a beet."

"Bite me." It was a weak comeback, and they both knew it.

"You don't need me for that—sounds like you've already found someone." Adam signaled to the bartender for a beer as well. "Come on, spill. Did you meet her at Bingham Brothers? I didn't think they hired anyone under the age of sixty."

Since the Bingham audit was still confidential, Dane fudged the truth a bit. "I didn't meet her at work. Sugar introduced us."

Adam's eyes widened. "She's Sugar's friend? Does she dance at Frisky's, too?" Adam backpedaled at Dane's frown. "Not that there's anything wrong with that. I mean, look at where your sister got her start. Not stripping, I mean. But making stripper clothes… I'll drink my beer now and shut up."

"Thank you," Dane snapped. "Keeley's not a stripper, she's an accountant. Sugar's accountant."

"Okay, sorry, Dane." He wrinkled his black brows. "Sugar's accountant? I think she might know Bridget."

"Maybe." Dane shrugged, still not eager to trot Keeley out for his sister's approval. He was a private kind of guy and besides, he and Keeley were just having some fun while their project lasted.

"Well, if you and she are still together in August, you can bring her home to Wisconsin for our wedding."

Dane flinched, and Adam hooted. "Boy, now you're white as a sheet. Okay, I can understand if she's not the type of girl you bring home to Momma. Believe me, I've been in that boat. Not that you can tell your sister that, though."

"It's not that. Keeley's great. She's smart, nice, beautiful. She even gives most of her money to her younger sister to help put her through college. Mom and Dad would love her."

"So what's the problem?"

"That *is* the problem. They'd start planning *my* wedding for next summer. All of us married and settled down. Stuck forever in one place."

Adam drank his beer and stared ahead thoughtfully. Dane wished he'd never broached the subject. Finally Adam broke the silence. "Would that be so terrible?"

"What?" Dane's eyes widened. "Marry Keeley? Are you nuts? You've got weddings on the brain again."

"I guess if you loved her, it wouldn't be nuts."

"Love? Who said anything about love?"

"*You're* the guy sitting in a bar with a sappy look on your face. When will you see her next?"

"Seven-forty-five tonight," Dane responded promptly and glared at Adam when he laughed.

"And how many minutes until then?"

Another seventy-five minutes. "Oh, can it. I'm *not* in love with her."

Adam watched him for a minute and shrugged. "Love's the thing, bro. Without it, we are clanging gongs." He stood and patted Dane's shoulder. "I have to go meet Bridget. Take care."

"Thanks a lot, buddy!" Dane called after him sarcastically. "And you can stop misquoting your wedding Scripture readings to me, too!"

Just then a metallic crash came from the bar's kitchen. Dane flinched again. *Gong.*

DANE FLIPPED THROUGH the packet of papers his P.I. had couriered over regarding the investigation into Adult Home Care of Chicago and its possible owner, Amanda Hobson. He pressed his lips together as the evidence mounted and pushed the intercom button on his desk. "Cherry, can you come in here?"

"Be right there," she said briskly.

Dane had no idea how Keeley did it all—a complicated secret audit plus enough of her executive assistant duties to not raise any eyebrows. She was amazing.

She appeared in the door and his mouth grew dry. Today she was wearing a hot pink top that should have clashed with her wig, but didn't. Her black skirt ended several inches above the *pièce de résistance,* a pair of thigh-high black leather boots with skinny heels that made her look like a pirate queen. Booty indeed.

"Ahoy—I mean, oh, hi, come on in and close the door."

She gave him a peculiar look at his verbal slip but did as he asked. "What's up, Dane?"

Nothing she should take care of at the office. "The investigator had these dropped off. Take a look." He passed her the packet.

She flipped through the papers and laughed triumphantly. "I *told* you it was her. The mysterious cash transfers, living beyond her means. And did you see the name on the business license for that phony home health-care agency? She loathes Binky and his grandson and this is the best way she can screw them over. When can we take the evidence to Binky?"

"Not for a couple of days. He has a board meeting in London, so he flew over there last night. I have the P.I. and his staff tailing Amanda in case she tries to leave town."

"Rats! All that work, and now we have to wait." She stood and paced across his office. "She's been ripping off the clients for two years, so I guess two days won't make a huge difference."

He smiled at her. She was so smart. "You called it right—I guess you win our bet."

"Bet?" She remembered and started to blush. "Oh. Five million dollars."

"Or a million kisses," he murmured, enjoying how her blush covered her lovely breasts. "You'll have to take an IOU for now. Once I start, I wouldn't want to stop."

Her hot green gaze met his and fell to the gleaming wood expanse of his desk, and he groaned, his cock hardening at the mental image of her flat on her back, boots wrapped around his waist as he pounded into her. He tried not to whimper. "Oh, Keeley, don't look at me like that. I'm not made of stone."

A sly smile spread over her face. "Care to make a bet on that?"

He shook his head ruefully. "No. You know I'd lose right now. Come on, talk to me about spreadsheets or something numerical. I have a meeting with Charlie in five minutes and I don't want to scare the poor guy."

"He'd be jealous because he doesn't measure up."

"Okay, that's helping."

Keeley beckoned him closer. "I learned where Charlie Bingham's cash has been going for the past several months."

"Where?" The devilish expression on her face clued him in that it was probably a good story.

"That money is going for the care and raising of Charles Andrew Bingham the Seventh."

Dane's jaw dropped. "Charlie has a son?"

"Apparently he's about seven months old. His mother is, or rather used to be, a feature dancer at Hot to Trot Gentlemen's Club in Louisville, Kentucky. She traced Charlie through the Bingham Brothers Web site and the boy passed a DNA test."

"His mother is a stripper?" Dane roared with

laughter. "After all the grief Charlie's given Binky over the years, he gets stuck with a stripper for the mother of the Bingham heir."

Keeley gave him a sour look.

He backpedaled, knowing her affection for Sugar. "Not that she's a bad person or anything. She could have gone to the papers, so she must hold her son's well-being first, like any good mother."

Keeley's expression lightened, so he knew he'd said the right thing.

"Are you busy after work today?" The sight of her footwear reminded him—he wanted to play pirate with her. She shook her head, and he couldn't miss the gleam in her eyes. "My place. Seven o'clock. Wear those boots and prepare to be boarded."

KEELEY DRAGGED herself into the office two days later. Lacey had come back to Chicago late Sunday and had kept her awake telling the stories of her Wisconsin adventures. Lucky Lacey could sleep 'til noon if she wanted, but Cherry the secretary had to drag her butt in at eight.

Oh, great, the crowd of losers was flocking around her desk again. They hadn't been around since Dane had marked his territory, so to speak. They turned and grinned when they saw her, but didn't move. "Excuse me."

"Hi, Cherry." Dirk from accounting smirked. "We thought you were a sweet cherry, but maybe you're a tart." The other men sniggered.

"What?" Something had gone wrong. Dane, where was Dane?

Dirk continued, "Somebody left this naughty photo

in the men's room this morning, and we were amazed to see it was you." He brandished a full-color poster, and the office swirled dizzily around Keeley. It was an old publicity photo from the Love Shack that she had allowed them to take before she wised up to the games some men played.

Cherry Tarte, the Love Shack's newest sensation, the lettering read. The photo had her in her red wig, whipped cream sprayed on her breasts and G-string and two maraschino cherries perched over where her nipples would be. Dammit, she thought she'd gotten rid all of those photos.

His sidekick started singing, "Boom-ba-dah boom, ba-da boom."

The men laughed and made cracks about her body and wondered aloud what she looked like under the whipped cream. "Get lost!" She hated how her voice shrilled, but she hadn't even felt this exposed dancing mostly naked at a strip bar.

"What the hell's going on here?" Dane's baritone bellowed through the office.

Keeley sagged with relief as Dane came striding toward her. Most of the hangers-on slunk away, but the ringleader brandished the poster. "Look, Weiss, you've got your very own stripper. You lucky dog, I bet she sure knows her moves when she goes—"

"Shut up and give me that poster. I'm not going to ask you again."

Dirk backed away, waving it in front of Dane's face. "Why? You already know what she looks like under whipped cream."

Dane reddened with rage but his voice was still low

and steady. "Fine. Keep it. It's as close as you'll ever get to a real woman anyway."

Dirk dropped the poster and punched wildly at Dane, who easily blocked it and laid into Dirk with a fist of his own.

The remaining men dispersed quickly at the sight of the jerk's lip pouring blood. "Weith, you thon-of-a-bitch!" Dirk lisped.

"Get your ass out of here or the next one's to your nose." Dane brandished his clenched hand, the streaks of blood a savage contrast to his fine cotton cuffs and gold cuff links, and Dirk left the office.

Keeley approached Dane cautiously, as he was staring at the poster on her desk. "Dane, are you all right?"

He shook his head and snorted without looking at her.

"Dane? Sweetheart?" She had never called him by any endearments in the office before.

"Why are you asking me if I'm all right?" He straightened and spun toward her. "You're the one who was under attack. You're all right, aren't you?" His muscles flexed and bunched under his suit jacket.

"Yes. Just a little scared."

"A little? Keeley, they were completely out of line."

She couldn't stand that poisonous poster. "So what? I'm used to it. See?" She pointed to her old photo.

"That really is you?" His face sagged. "I thought it might be one of those computer-altered things posted to stir up trouble."

"It's stirring up trouble all right, but it's real. That was me about seven years ago. Remember that place I worked to put myself through school? It was the Love Shack strip club, and I was their top act. Miss Cherry Tarte. Whipped cream, maraschinos, the whole bit. I danced naked for men, took their money, and was glad to do it."

"What? After all the grief you got with your mom's pervert boyfriends? How could you do that?"

"My terms!" She stabbed a thumb into her breast-bone, ignoring the ache building underneath. "My rules. If I didn't want to give some scumbag a lap dance, I didn't. If I didn't want to do bachelor parties, I didn't. And don't tell me you've never been a customer because I *know* you have."

Dane winced guiltily. The phone on her desk rang, and he answered. Charlie Bingham's angry voice blared. Dane listened for a few seconds and cut him off. "Look, Bingham, I've already punched one guy today, so busting you in the chops won't make any difference to me and I'll derive intense pleasure from it. I'll take care of it if you shut up and hang up." Dane slammed the phone.

Keeley didn't need to ask what that was about.

"Your…posters…are everywhere in the office—all the bathrooms, copy rooms, lunchrooms. There's no way you can stay here today. I'll take you down in the freight elevator and you can take the rest of the day off. Binky won't be back until tomorrow. His meeting ran over." His tone was cool and impersonal.

Her shoulders sagged. So much for Dane. He couldn't handle the fact she'd been a stripper. "No, don't bother taking me in the freight elevator. I'll walk out the front door. I may have taken off my clothes for money, but I still have my pride."

KEELEY WAS ABLE to keep her composure all the way home and up the stairs into her apartment. She tiptoed past Lacey's sleeping form on the futon and made it into her bedroom before glimpsing herself in the pier mirror. Floozy red hair, spidery-looking fake eyelashes and clothes that would make a whore blush. She yanked off the wig and eyelashes, chucking them across the room. Her strappy red heels, Dane's favorites, followed shortly. Dane. She flung herself on the bed and burst into tears. What did a girl from a trailer park expect? Wine and roses? More like beer and dandelions.

"Hey, hey, what's wrong?" Lacey stood behind her in the doorway, rubbing sleep from her eyes. "Are you hurt? Did you get fired?"

Keeley could only shake her head and weep into her uncomforting comforter. Lacey shook her head in dismay and sat next to her, gently removing her hair pins and rubbing her scalp. "Talk to me, sis. Is it Dane?"

Oh, it was Dane, all right. She had a fresh wave of tears. "It's Dane, it's me, it's everything." She was sick of deceiving Dane, sick of deceiving her loyal sister, sick of deceiving herself that she was actually going to be someone someday. That she would actually be valued for herself as a whole person, not just her body.

"Tell me." Lacey flipped her onto her back with a martial arts move. "Now."

"Lacey, I'm not who you think I am," she began painfully. "I've done things I'm not necessarily proud of."

Lacey sat on her heels and sighed. "Oh, Keeley. Are you beating yourself up over your exotic-dancing job?"

Keeley propped herself on her elbows and gaped at her. "What? How long have you known?"

"About five years now." Lacey shifted to a cross-legged

position on the bed, a sympathetic expression on her face. "Remember when I was starting high school and you came to visit? You still had that old clunker of a car and the backseat was a mess. You offered me five bucks to clean it and I found a flyer from that place in the city, that club."

"The Love Shack?" Lacey nodded and Keeley shifted onto one elbow and groaned.

"I wondered why you would have something like that in your car, so I checked it online. They had a picture on the Web site—I recognized you despite your wig and, um, outfit."

Keeley started to cry again, realizing it probably had been the same raunchy publicity photo that was currently making the rounds at Bingham Brothers. "You were the one person in the world who I never wanted to find out." Dane had been the second. "But you never said a word."

Her sister pulled her into a hug. "You didn't seem any different to me, so I figured you were okay with it."

Keeley relaxed into her sister's embrace, putting her thoughts into words for the first time. "I *was* okay with it, except for not being honest about it with you. I got a job as a cocktail waitress at a regular bar. One of my friends worked at the Love Shack and convinced me to apply. Once I learned how much money she made, I auditioned and never looked back."

"Makes sense, Keel. Chicago is pricey."

"And all my money was going for books and tuition at the city college." She sighed into Lacey's shoulder. "I had been living in a neighborhood even worse than the trailer park, Lacey. That's why I never wanted you to come visit me."

"Oh, Keeley." Her sister stroked her hair. "You should have stopped sending money home to me for karate. I would have understood."

"No, Lacey." Keeley pushed away from her sister and peered into her green eyes, almost a match for Keeley's own. "You needed those self-defense classes. I didn't trust Mom not to keep bringing losers around who might have bothered you, like they did me."

Lacey gave her a wicked smile. "One did try to *bother* me, as you put it. I gave him a knife-hand chop to the throat and he passed out on the floor."

Keeley gasped, but Lacey just laughed. "I called 911, and the cops arrested him and took him to the hospital—something about a fractured larynx. After that, Mom's social life took a definite downturn. Seems all the local perverts have their own grapevine." She patted Keeley's hand. "So all your karate money was well worthwhile."

Keeley stared at her, aghast. "You never told me any of that! How could you keep me in the dark?"

"Like you did, sis?"

Keeley finally laughed. "*Touché*, sis. No more secrets between us."

"And no more secrets between you and Dane." Lacey gave her a stern look. "That's why you're crying, isn't it? You kept the exotic dancing a secret and he was all shocked and you probably got all angry with him and now you're all upset because you think you've lost him forever."

Keeley needed a second to follow that sentence but had to agree with it. "The look on his face. Like he has any right to judge me. He's probably spent more time in strip clubs than I have." She briefly explained the unpleasant events of the morning.

Lacey wrinkled her brow. "So you two never actually had the chance to discuss anything?"

"He hustled me out the door like some one-night stand the morning after."

"Sounds like all hell was breaking loose and he wanted to get you clear of it," Lacey stated. "And wouldn't *you* be shocked if he told you he'd worked his way through school dancing naked for bachelorette parties?"

Keeley stared agape at her. The image of Dane in a leopard-print G-string being screamed at by drunken brides was too much for her, and she burst into giggles.

"See?" Lacey poked her in the side. "Cut the guy some slack. After all, you're in love with him."

"No, I'm not." Keeley frowned. "How could I be in love with a man who can't accept me for who I am?"

Lacey shoved her so she fell on the mattress. "How's he supposed to accept you for who you are? You never showed him who you are, you idiot! Honestly!" She rolled her eyes. "He'd never been here to your apartment, he had no idea you were dying to travel and see ballet performances, and you hadn't worked up the guts to tell him about Cherry Tarte. Face it, Keel. You wimped out."

Keeley slumped onto the edge of the bed. "Dane tried to dig deeper, to find the real me, but you're right— I chickened out."

"Is Dane worth opening yourself up or was he just buttering me up to get on your good side?"

"No, he's always like that—calls his mom every week and is best man at his sister's wedding this summer." Keeley sniffled. "He brought me homemade cherry pie and rubbed my feet after a long day in those awful shoes. Popped popcorn for me, let me hog the bed…" She stopped, her eyes wide. She'd let that one out of the bag.

Lacey just giggled. "I kinda figured you had more going on than good-night kisses."

Keeley felt her face heat. "Do what I say, not what I do."

Her sister waggled a finger at Keeley. "Then *you* do what *I* say and talk to the man. It's time for you to bare your soul now, not your body."

IT WAS A GRIM GROUP that met in the Bingham Brothers conference room the next day. Dane was heartsick that he'd screwed up things royally with Keeley and inadvertently exposed her to ridicule by letting her masquerade continue.

He looked around the table and saw Binky's haggard face and Charlie's worried one. The only thing that Charlie knew was there had been a major accounting discrepancy.

The corporate counsels and private investigator wore serious expressions. Mrs. Hobson was there as well, ostensibly to take notes, but she looked as if nothing in the world bothered her.

Keeley was not there. He'd left a message about the meeting on her voice mail, but she hadn't returned his call. He couldn't wait any longer for her. "Why don't we get started?"

The door opened and Keeley entered. Not Cherry, and not the buttoned-up beige Keeley he'd first met. Today she wore a well-tailored yet classy navy-blue business pantsuit with a white blouse underneath, along with fashionable but sensible blue heels. "Sorry I'm late. I got stuck in traffic."

Dane suppressed an inappropriate grin. "Gentlemen, this is Keeley Davis. Some of you may have already met her."

Charlie and Mrs. Hobson looked at her blankly.

Keeley smiled. "Hiya, Mrs. Hobson. How're ya doing?"

Dane relaxed a bit in his chair. With Keeley there, he could pull this off.

Keeley saw Dane settle back and take charge of the decidedly frosty atmosphere. His blue stare lasered through the older woman. *Go get her*, she silently cheered.

Dane fired the opening salvo. "Mrs. Hobson, we know about you and the special group of trust funds."

"Me? Mr. Bingham's grandfather entrusted them to him to care for since they belong to his elderly friends. Why? Is something wrong?" Her faded eyes widened inquisitively.

Binky and Charlie shuffled uneasily, sending accusatory looks their way. Amanda Hobson was good, Keeley had to admit. The role of loyal executive assistant fit her perfectly, except for the calculating gleam hidden deep in her eyes. Keeley doubted if the men could see it. Men almost always missed that.

But not Dane, apparently. He viewed Charlie's assistant with the same cool expression and didn't waver. He gestured to Keeley, who was sitting next to him. "And you *have* met Keeley Davis. She's the forensic accountant Binky hired to audit the trust funds."

"A forensic accountant?" Mrs. Hobson's brow wrinkled politely. "I don't believe I've had the pleasure."

"You probably wouldn't recognize me without my red wig and miniskirt," Keeley informed her.

"Cherry?" A crafty expression came over her face.

"You're right. The last I saw of you was in that poster, when you were wearing nothing but some whipped cream and a smile."

"That was nothing but a photo manipulation designed to embarrass her," Dane interjected.

Keeley rested her hand on his forearm. "No, Dane. No more lies. Not from me, and certainly not from her." She gave the older woman a hard stare. "That photo's real, as you must have known when you dug it up to embarrass me. I was a poor trailer park kid who paid my way through school as an exotic dancer."

The Bingham men yelped, Binky in delight and Charlie in dismay.

"So you admit it." Mrs. Hobson gave her a twisted smile.

"Of course." Keeley narrowed her eyes and threw down the gauntlet. "I earned my money honestly, not stealing it from Binky's long-standing friends."

Charlie looked between the two women. "Stealing from friends? Can someone tell me what's going on?"

Binky sighed. "Something was rotten in the state of Denmark, as the Bard said, so I brought Dane and Keeley in to discover if the young prince was the thief."

Charlie bolted to his feet, his chair tipping backward. "Me?" He thunked a thumb into his chest. "You thought *I* would steal from our clients? I'm no goddamn thief!"

Binky looked at him pleadingly. "Please, Charlie. I so hoped it wasn't you. But all the suspicious accounts were directly under your bailiwick."

"Because you specifically gave them to me! All your old cronies and their widows to look after. I knew they were important to you, so I made sure Mrs. Hobson here…kept an eye on them…." His anger deflated. "Oh, my God. Did I set the fox to guard the henhouse?"

"I'm sure I don't know what you're talking about," the older woman said primly, but Keeley detected a crack in her facade and brought out the pry bar.

"Adult Home Care of Chicago," Keeley announced and saw a small flinch. She passed copies of her audit results to Binky and Charlie. "You should have done your homework better, Amanda," she said, purposely using the woman's first name to psychologically level the playing field. "According to Mr. Bingham here, several of his friends are either too well or too sick to require home health care. So there was no legitimate reason for them to make payments to your ghost payrolling company.

Amanda scoffed. "Oooh, a ghost payrolling company. How unusual here in Chicago, but you can't tie me to anything." *I was too careful,* her expression smirked.

"Actually, yes we can," Dane chimed in. "As part of your employee agreement with Bingham Brothers, and according to federal regulations, as well, the company has a right to conduct periodic background checks. Making sure people aren't funneling money where it shouldn't be funneled." He pulled out another sheaf of papers. "Our investigator found several large regular transfers into your personal account."

"So?" She shrugged. "I inherited some money from my mother when she died a few years ago."

Keeley shook her head. "No, the only thing you got from your mother was the idea on how to bilk Bingham Brothers using a home health-care scam. You saw how much cash people were willing to pay to stay in their homes and took despicable advantage of that."

"Admit it, Amanda. Admit you stole the money." Binky stared at her. "Pay back our clients and I won't prosecute you."

"Sorry, Binky." She shrugged. "Even if I had stolen five million dollars, where do you think it would be? Under my bed? Any decent embezzler would have opened offshore accounts for this very purpose."

Dane's eyes narrowed and a cold smile crept across his face. "How did you know it was five million dollars, Amanda? Nobody mentioned that amount, and you haven't looked at the papers we gave the Binghams."

"What?" The crack widened, thanks to Dane's sharpness. "Didn't you say it was five million?"

"No." Keeley shook her head. "Give up. You've lost."

The older woman pursed her lips and laughed with a nasty hysterical edge. "Don't you think I already know that? I lost thirty years ago."

"Don't—" Binky said, casting a nervous look at Charlie.

"Don't what? Don't tell your grandson the truth?" She whipped around to Keeley. "Look what you started, you little tart. All this truth-telling." She shuddered theatrically. "God forbid, precious little Charles Bingham the Sixth should know the truth about his grandfather. And father."

"What *about* my father? He passed away thirty years ago. Grandfather, what's she talking about?" Charlie demanded.

Binky spread his hands helplessly, his face sagging. "Charlie, I'm so sorry. I never wanted you to know. Amanda and your father, well…"

Charlie snapped his head around to the woman he'd

thought had been loyal to him. "You and my father? You had an affair, didn't you?"

"No, it was more than an affair—I loved him!"

Keeley rolled her eyes. Loved the Bingham billions more likely, according to Binky's former secretary.

Amanda clasped her hands to her blouse. "Quint and I were soul mates. I fulfilled him in a way your mother never could."

Charlie slammed a fist onto the conference table, making the papers rattle. "You leave my mother out of it!"

She ignored his outburst and continued, "She was wrapped up in you, you little bastard, so your father turned to *me.* We were planning our new life together when he was tragically killed." She gave a dramatic sob.

Binky looked shell-shocked and Charlie was about to pop a blood vessel. Keeley stepped into the breach. "No, that's not true. Quint dumped you. Left you. Kicked you to the curb. And for what? Money. The Bingham money. Binky here wanted his grandson to have an intact family, so he threatened to cut off Quint's party-boy funds. Quint never loved you enough to be *poor.*"

Amanda's face crumpled and she buried it in her hands.

"But…but…I can't believe that she would wait all these years for payback." Charlie dropped into a chair. "Do you have any real proof?"

Dane silently slid a piece of paper over to him, a sympathetic look on his face.

Charlie read the paper, his expression slumping into lines of anguish. "The business license to Adult Home Care of Chicago," he said dully. "Mandy Quinton, proprietor." He stared at the older woman. "My father wouldn't give you his name, so you stole that, too."

"Quint always called me Mandy." Amanda coolly stared at him. "Bingham Brothers owes me, and you would have kept on paying if it weren't for this slut with more boobs than brains."

Dane growled deep in his throat.

Keeley stood and leaned over the table to Amanda, their faces inches apart. "First of all, a woman who had an adulterous affair is in no position to throw stones. And second, I may have nice breasts, but I have even better brains. More than enough to catch *you.*"

KEELEY SLIPPED OUT while Binky, Dane and the lawyers were discussing the repercussions to the company. She desperately wanted to talk to Dane, but now wasn't the time. She took the elevator to the lobby and was pushing her way through the revolving doors when she heard Dane call her name.

"Keeley, wait!" He ran after her.

"Dane." Her heart thumped. She hadn't planned this, she wasn't ready for him despite her brave talk with Lacey. "Don't they need you upstairs?"

He shook his head. "You and I have done our part. The rest is up to Binky and the legal staff."

She looked along noisy, busy LaSalle Street, heart of the financial district and where she'd always wanted to be. But LaSalle Street was no place for laying her heart bare. "Do you want to go for a drink?"

He shook his head. "I've had enough of being trapped inside. Let's catch a cab to the lakefront for some fresh air."

She agreed. Maybe the natural beauty would boost her courage. Dane hailed a taxi and soon they were walking along Lake Michigan. He tipped his handsome face up to the clear blue sky. "Ah, much better. Sometimes I wonder why I picked a career that keeps me inside most of the time."

"Why *did* you pick business consulting, Dane?" She shed her suit jacket in the hot May sun, and Dane gallantly carried it for her.

"I love the puzzle of it," he explained. "Figuring out what, or who, should go where. What to do with a company." He laughed. "Plus, my family would tell you I'm too bullheaded to easily work for anyone else. How about you?"

"I love order." She put her words together carefully, knowing they would reveal something about her she'd never shared before. "I guess because I grew up in chaos. And I was a champion couch-diver. Any change that fell between the cushions went into my piggy bank and I even had an old checkbook register to add every coin."

"An accountant in the making." Dane glanced at her. "So what happens when something comes along to overturn your sense of order?"

Like a certain gorgeous Wisconsin financial consultant? She wanted to take his hand but was unsure how he would react. She decided to talk business instead. It was always safer. "That meeting this afternoon was certainly chaotic. Do you think Binky will prosecute her?" Keeley asked.

"Mmm, I doubt it. He'll probably pay back the accounts himself."

Keeley gaped at him and laughed. "I guess five million's a drop in the bucket for him." The lake breeze tossed her hair, her real hair, and she was glad for its coolness on her scalp. She wouldn't throw away her wig, but would be perfectly happy to keep it in the closet for a long time.

"A small price to pay for peace of mind. He doesn't want all the sordid details about Quint to come out, for Charlie's sake."

"And for the company's sake," Keeley reminded him. "If word got out, the clients might panic."

"That, too," Dane agreed. "Binky offered me the controller position on a permanent basis. I told him I'd think about it."

She grimaced. "Why would you want to work there? It's stuck in the 1950s and you can't think Charlie Bingham will be any happier to work with you after what he learned today."

Dane moved off the wide concrete path and pulled her to a tree-shaded bench, away from marauding bicyclists and zoned-out joggers. He rested his elbow on the bench's arm. "I'm considering taking the job so I can stay here in Chicago."

Her heart flipped in her chest but she forced herself to calmly ask, "Why? To be near your sister and her fiancé?"

"No, Keeley." He took a deep breath. "So I can be near *you*."

"Me?" she whispered, shocked despite all her hopes.

"Yes, you." Now that he'd said it, he relaxed his shoulders and took her hand. "What do you say to that?" He tugged her close.

She pressed her face into his warm chest and inhaled his wonderfully familiar scent.

"Keeley, sweetheart?" He held her face, his blue eyes a dead match for the horizon. "What do you think? Do you want me around?"

"For how long?"

"How long do you want me?" He kissed her gently. "You have to know I don't think less of you for your dancing gigs. God knows I dropped at least enough money in those places to pay for some girl's textbooks."

She giggled at his joke but grew serious. "Dane, the look on your face when you saw the poster, though."

"Keeley, I'd walked in to see a mob of men hassling you and that scared me. I almost tore them apart and then I saw a photo of you wearing whipped cream and two maraschinos. My mental state was not the best at that point. All I could think about was making sure you were somewhere safe, and that wasn't Bingham Brothers."

"That's what Lacey said," she admitted. "She told me to cut you some slack."

He grinned. "Your sister's one smart cookie. But how could she not be? You raised her, didn't you?"

"Pretty much," she admitted. "We had each other, and that was enough."

"But now she's grown, and you need more, don't you, Keeley? You need me. And I need you." He swallowed hard. "It's more than need, baby. I love you."

"Oh, Dane." To her embarrassment, tears filled her eyes, blurring his features into a watery silhouette. She swiped at the moisture. "Darn it, why am I always crying around you? I never cry this much."

"You are always safe with me, Keeley. That's why."

She was safe, so she took a deep breath and gathered her soggy courage. "I love you, too, Dane. Ever since the coffee shop, it's been building with every thoughtful gesture you made, every time you loved me. I just didn't admit it because I didn't want to need anyone."

He covered her face in passionate kisses, leaving them both breathless and aroused. He plunged his fingers through her hair and kissed the top of her head. "You've haunted my dreams since we met, and I wake up to find reality even better. I can't stand to be away from you, Keeley."

She grinned at him. "Then for goodness' sake, don't take Binky's job. If you still want to travel, I want to go with you. My clients can e-mail me their accounting files, and I'll come back for tax season."

"Really? You want to travel with me?"

"Dane, I've only been to two states—Illinois and Missouri."

"Not even Wisconsin?" he gasped in mock horror.

"Not even Wisconsin."

"We'll fix that because I want to take you home to meet my family." He nuzzled her ear and whispered, "I thought we could announce our engagement."

She pulled back in shock, examining his expression for any hint of joking. He was as serious as she'd ever seen him, and he nodded. "Marry me, Keeley. I want your sister to walk you down the aisle while my brothers stand with me. I want everybody to see how right we are together."

They *were* right together. "Only one condition."

He held himself very still, waiting for her answer. "What?"

"You absolutely have to let me give you some dance lessons for our wedding reception. Otherwise it will look like I'm dancing around you like you're a strip club pole bolted to the floor."

He threw back his head and laughed. "Baby, you can use me for your pole anytime."

She laughed and laughed in delight, feeling as if she were floating among the tops of the trees but still firmly with Dane. He was her rock, more solid than the boulders lining the shore and more powerful than the waves crashing the beach. "I love you, Dane Weiss, but you never did tell me your middle name. I'm not sure I can marry a man without knowing his middle name."

"Keeley…" He grimaced.

"Come on, you know I'll see it on the marriage license." She tickled him in the ribs.

"Herbert," he muttered. "My grandfather's name."

"Herbert?" She stifled a smile. "I love you, Dane Herbert Weiss. Forever."

"And I love you, too, Keeley… What's your middle name?" he prodded.

She sighed. "Loretta."

"Loretta?" He bit his lip but those cute dimples showed his amusement. "Is that a family name?"

"If you must know, my mother is a country music fan and I was named after Loretta Lynn. I'm just grateful my full name isn't Loretta Lynn Davis."

"I'll never mention it again as long as you never call me Herbert."

"Deal." She sealed it with a kiss. "Remember our bet? You owe me a million kisses," she teased him.

"Well, then, I guess I better get started." But they were grinning too much to kiss and rested their foreheads against each other, their love as soothing as the cool lake breeze and as comforting as the warm sun above them.

Epilogue

"HAVING A GOOD TIME?" Dane called to Keeley as she whirled by in his father's arms at Bridget's wedding reception. Keeley nodded and laughed, her eyes sparkling. Bob Weiss was the undisputed local polka king and had eagerly offered to show a trained dancer like Keeley the steps.

She, of course, had picked them up easy as pie and had impressed his family with much more than her dance skills. Despite the hard work leading to Bridget's wedding in their Wisconsin hometown, every single member of his family had taken the time to pull him aside at some point to compliment Keeley. Of course, Bridget, Colin and Adam had been sure to point out he in no way deserved her, but that was okay. He knew that already.

Bridget stood on the edge of the dance floor laughing with her new husband, not minding in the least Keeley was getting all the attention. Keeley had joined a modern dance troupe, and while some performances were a bit avant-garde for Dane's tastes, he could tell she enjoyed herself immensely, and that was good enough for him.

The polka band wheezed to a finish and Dane's dad returned Keeley. "Thanks for letting me dance with your girl, son." He patted her shoulder. "You're as good as those professional ballroom dancers on TV that Dane's mom likes to watch. I'll ask the band to play another polka later on so I can dance with little Lacey."

"She'll look forward to it." She smiled at Dane's dad, obviously pleased her sister had found easy acceptance. The bandleader caught Dane's eye and nodded.

"Come on, honey." He took her hand and pulled her over to a quiet corner. The band started playing his special request that had cost him a couple of twenties slipped to the leader. He would have paid much more if necessary.

"Listen, Dane!" She clutched his hand. "They're playing 'Wooden Heart.'"

The band's singer began singing an English translation of the original folk song that Dane had given him and Keeley's eyes widened as she understood the words for the first time. "Dane, is that right? You were singing the same thing in German? How you would always come back to me and you'd always be true to me?"

"Yes." Dane knew what the third verse would say. "Listen to this part."

Her eyes filled. "'In a year, when the grapes are ripe on the vine, my bride you'll be and then it's yours I will be.' Dane, you sang this to me the night I fell in love with you. When you cracked my wooden heart."

"And you cracked mine." He dropped to one knee and popped open the ring box he'd secretly carried from Chicago. "Be my bride before the year ends, Keeley. *Lieber Schatz, i' bleib dir treu.* My sweetheart, I stay true to you."

She gasped and covered her mouth. "Oh, Dane, I'll stay true to you always." She pulled the ring out of its black velvet lining. "It's lovely. But you told me we'd go ring-shopping after Bridget's wedding was over."

"I couldn't wait any longer," he confessed as he slipped it on her finger. "It's a cognac-colored diamond with white diamonds around it in a gold band. At least that's what the jeweler said. I picked it because the stone is warm and beautiful—like you."

Keeley pulled him to his feet and threw her arms around his neck. "I love you, Dane Weiss."

"And I love you, Keeley Davis." He kissed her in giddy relief, only noticing the music had stopped when he heard a giggle behind him.

"I think it worked, Mom," his sister stage-whispered.

Dane groaned. So much for privacy. Keeley let go of him as if he were suddenly electrified. "We, um, we just, um…" she trailed off, hanging back in embarrassment.

"I gave Keeley her engagement ring," he finished and ducked as she was engulfed in a mob of female relatives.

Lacey was first to hug and squeal but his sequin-clad mom was a close second. "Oh, Dane, two more daughters for me!"

"Two?" He was momentarily confused.

"Keeley and Lacey, of course." She hugged them both with her cushiony, comforting arms. "Welcome to the Weiss family, girls. You'll have to call me Mom now."

The tears flowed freely after that and even Dane blinked a couple extra times.

"Something in your eye?" Adam had sidled next to him.

"Shut up." He slugged Adam's shoulder, and his new brother-in-law slugged him back.

"I told you, bro. Love's the thing." Adam admired his

new wife, and Dane admired Keeley as she tossed back her head and laughed with sheer joy. She met his gaze and blew him a kiss.

All Dane's hopes, dreams and longings were wrapped up in that beautiful, wonderful, sexy woman, and he knew she would make all of them come true. "You know, Adam, for once you're right. Love *is* the thing."

* * * * *

*The editors at Harlequin Blaze
have never been afraid to push the limits—
tempting readers with the forbidden,
whetting their appetites with a
wide variety of story lines.
But now we're breaking the final barrier—
the time barrier.*

*In July, watch for
BOUND TO PLEASE
by fan favorite Hope Tarr,
Harlequin Blaze's first ever
historical romance—
a story that's truly
Blaze-worthy in every sense.*

Here's a sneak peek…

BRIANNA STRETCHED OUT beside Ewan, languid as a cat, and promptly fell asleep. Midday sunshine streamed into the chamber, bathing her lovely, long-limbed body in golden light, the sea-scented breeze wafting inside to dry the damp red-gold tendrils curling about her flushed face. Propping himself up on one elbow, Ewan slid his gaze over her. She looked beautiful and whole, satisfied and sated, and altogether happier than he had so far seen her. A slight smile curved her beautiful lips as though she must be in the midst of a lovely dream. She'd molded her lush, lovely body to his and laid her head in the curve of his shoulder and settled in to sleep beside him. For the longest while he lay there turned toward her, content to watch her sleep, at near perfect peace.

Not wholly perfect, for she had yet to answer his marriage proposal. Still, she wanted to make a baby with him, and Ewan no longer viewed her plan as the travesty he once had. He wanted children—sons to carry on after him, though a bonny little daughter with flame-colored hair would be nice, too. But he also wanted more than to simply plant his seed and be on his way. He wanted to lie beside Brianna night upon night as she increased, rub soothing unguents into the swell of her belly, knead the ache from her back and make slow, gentle love to her. He wanted to hold his newly born child in his arms and look down into Brianna's tired but radiant face and blot the perspiration from her brow and be a husband to her in every way.

He gave her a gentle nudge. "Brie?"

"Hmmm?"

She rolled onto her side and he captured her against his chest. One arm wrapped about her waist, he bent to her ear and asked, "Do you think we might have just made a baby?"

Her eyes remained closed, but he felt her tense against him. "I don't know. We'll have to wait and see."

He stroked his hand over the flat plane of her belly. "You're so small and tight it's hard to imagine you increasing."

"All women increase no matter how large or small they start out. I may not grow big as a croft, but I'll be big enough, though I have hopes I may not waddle like a duck, at least not too badly."

The reference to his fair-day teasing was not lost on him. He grinned. "Brianna MacLeod grown so large she must sit still for once in her life. I'll need the proof of my own eyes to believe it."

Despite their banter, he felt his spirits dip. Assuming they were so blessed, he wouldn't have the chance to see her thus. By then he would be long gone, restored to his clan according to the sad bargain they'd struck. He opened his mouth to ask her to marry him again and then clamped it closed, not wanting to spoil the moment, but the unspoken words weighed like a millstone on his heart.

The damnable bargain they'd struck was proving to be a devil's pact indeed.

* * * * *

Will these two star-crossed lovers
find their sexily-ever-after?
Find out in
BOUND TO PLEASE
by Hope Tarr,
available in July wherever
Harlequin® Blaze™ books are sold.

Harlequin Blaze marks new territory with its first historical novel!

For years readers have trusted the Harlequin Blaze series to entertain them with a variety of stories— Now Blaze is breaking down the final barrier— the time barrier!

Welcome to Blaze Historicals—all the sexiness you love in a Blaze novel, all the adventure of a historical romance. It's the best of both worlds!

Don't miss the first book in this exciting new miniseries:

BOUND TO PLEASE
by Hope Tarr

New laird Brianna MacLeod knows she can't protect her land or her people without a man by her side. So what else can she do—she kidnaps one! Only, she doesn't expect to find herself the one enslaved....

**Available in July
wherever Harlequin books are sold.**

www.eHarlequin.com   HB79411

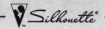

SPECIAL EDITION™

NEW YORK TIMES
BESTSELLING AUTHOR

DIANA PALMER

A brand-new Long, Tall Texans novel

HEART OF STONE

Feeling unwanted and unloved, Keely returns
to Jacobsville and to Boone Sinclair, a rancher
troubled by his own past. Boone has always
seemed reserved, but now Keely discovers a
sensuality with him that quickly turns to love. Can
they each see past their own scars to let love in?

*Available September 2008
wherever you buy books.*

REQUEST YOUR FREE BOOKS!

2 FREE NOVELS PLUS 2 FREE GIFTS!

HARLEQUIN®

Blaze™

Red-hot reads!

YES! Please send me 2 FREE Harlequin® Blaze™ novels and my 2 FREE gifts (gifts are worth about $10). After receiving them, if I don't wish to receive any more books, I can return the shipping statement marked "cancel." If I don't cancel, I will receive 6 brand-new novels every month and be billed just $4.24 per book in the U.S. or $4.71 per book in Canada, plus 25¢ shipping and handling per book and applicable taxes, if any*. That's a savings of 15% or more off the cover price! I understand that accepting the 2 free books and gifts places me under no obligation to buy anything. I can always return a shipment and cancel at any time. Even if I never buy another book, the two free books and gifts are mine to keep forever.

151 HDN ERVA 351 HDN ERUX

Name	(PLEASE PRINT)	
Address		Apt. #
City	State/Prov.	Zip/Postal Code

Signature (if under 18, a parent or guardian must sign)

Mail to the **Harlequin Reader Service:**
IN U.S.A.: P.O. Box 1867, Buffalo, NY 14240-1867
IN CANADA: P.O. Box 609, Fort Erie, Ontario L2A 5X3

Not valid to current subscribers of Harlequin Blaze books.

Want to try two free books from another line?
Call 1-800-873-8635 or visit www.morefreebooks.com.

* Terms and prices subject to change without notice. N.Y. residents add applicable sales tax. Canadian residents will be charged applicable provincial taxes and GST. Offer not valid in Quebec. This offer is limited to one order per household. All orders subject to approval. Credit or debit balances in a customer's account(s) may be offset by any other outstanding balance owed by or to the customer. Please allow 4 to 6 weeks for delivery. Offer available while quantities last.

Your Privacy: Harlequin Books is committed to protecting your privacy. Our Privacy Policy is available online at www.eHarlequin.com or upon request from the Reader Service. From time to time we make our lists of customers available to reputable third parties who may have a product or service of interest to you. If you would prefer we not share your name and address, please check here. ☐

HB08R

Silhouette®

Romantic
SUSPENSE

Sparked by Danger,
Fueled by Passion.

Conard County: The Next Generation

When he learns the truth about his father, military
man Ethan Parish is determined to reunite with his
long-lost family in Wyoming. On his way into town,
he clashes with policewoman Connie Halloran,
whose captivating beauty entices him. When
Connie's daughter is threatened, Ethan must use
his military skills to keep her safe. Together they
race against time to find the little girl and confront
the dangers inherent in family secrets.

Look for

A Soldier's Homecoming

by *New York Times*
bestselling author
Rachel Lee

Available in July wherever you buy books.

Visit Silhouette Books at www.eHarlequin.com   SRS27589

HARLEQUIN®

Blaze™

COMING NEXT MONTH

#405 WHAT I DID ON MY SUMMER VACATION
Thea Divine, Debbi Rawlins, Samantha Hunter
A Sizzling Summer Collection
Three single women end up with a fling worth writing about in this Blazing summer collection. Whether they spend their time in the city, in the woods or at the beach, their reports are bound to be strictly X-rated!

#406 INCOGNITO Kate Hoffmann
Forbidden Fantasies
Haven't you ever wished you could be someone else? Lily Hart has. So when she's mistaken for a promiscuous celebrity, she jumps at the chance to live out the erotic lifestyle she's always envied. After all, nobody will find out. Or will they?

#407 BOUND TO PLEASE Hope Tarr
Blaze Historicals
Blaze marks new territory with its first historical novel! New laird Brianna MacLeod knows she can't protect her land or her people without a man by her side. So, she kidnaps one! Only, she never expects to find herself the one enslaved....

#408 HEATED RUSH Leslie Kelly
The Wrong Bed: Again and Again
Annie Davis is in trouble. Her big family reunion is looming, and she needs a stand-in man—fast. Her solution? Bachelor number twenty at the charity bachelor auction. But there's more to her rent-a-date than meets the eye....

#409 BED ON ARRIVAL Kelley St. John
The Sixth Sense
Jenee Vicknair is keeping a wicked secret. Every night she has wild, mind-blowing sex with a perfect stranger. They never exchange words—their bodies say everything that needs to be said. If only her lover didn't vanish into thin air the moment the satisfaction was over....

#410 FLASHPOINT Jill Shalvis
American Heroes: The Firefighters
Zach Thomas might put out fires for a living, but when the sexy firefighter meets EMT Brooke O'Brian, all he wants to do is stoke her flames. Still, can Brooke count on him to take the heat if the sparks between them flare out of control?

www.eHarlequin.com

HBCNM0608